The Love That Lingers

Maya

notionpress.com

INDIA · SINGAPORE · MALAYSIA

ISBN 979-8-89906-283-4

CONTENTS

THE WEIGHT OF THE DAY, THE ILLUSION OF EASE

Mornings at home were always a blur. Between juggling breakfast, misplaced keys, and last-minute wardrobe crises, I barely had time to breathe. The clock ticked louder with each passing second, pushing me out the door with a travel mug in hand and a mental to-do list already half-completed.

But once I was in the car, everything shifted. Driving had always been my quiet reset. Even with traffic crawling and horns creating their usual morning racket, there was something grounding about being behind the wheel. I liked the feel of the road, the familiar turns, the steady rhythm of movement.

With music filling the car, it felt less like a commute and more like a small escape—a buffer zone between the chaos at home and the demands waiting at the office. A space that was entirely mine, if only for a little while.

By the time I reached the office, the building already buzzed with life. I settled into my desk, skimming through a mountain of emails, fingers flying across the keyboard while the phone rang off the hook. My headset perched on one ear, I toggled between conversations and task lists, my voice calm even as my mind spun with deadlines.

By mid-morning, I finally allowed myself a breather. Rising from my desk, I stretched the stiffness from my shoulders and made my way toward the break room, the promise of coffee pulling me forward. The day had been relentless.

"Good morning!" I chirped as I passed Ryan's desk, watching him jolt awake from a half-hearted nap. His sheepish grin made me laugh, and just like that, the morning felt a little lighter, a little more bearable. I made my rounds, weaving through the labyrinth of cubicles, sprinkling jokes and casual compliments like confetti. It was my ritual, my way of setting the tone, of making the day seem a little less heavy for everyone.

I wore cheerfulness like a second skin, always the one to speak first. The woman who always knew how to make people smile. But sometimes… I get quiet. I slip away from the crowd—not because I want to, but because I need to. And I know, some people take that as distance. Or worse. They think I'm pulling away, shutting them out.

When I finally settled back at my desk. I thrived in the madness, in the noise and busyness, in the buzz of constant chatter. It felt good to be needed, to be useful, to be the one people relied on. The hours blurred together, the office buzzing with life, with laughter, with people constantly passing by my desk, asking for help, asking for favours, asking for my time. And I gave it all away freely. Because it felt good to be needed.

But even within the madness, there were pockets of warmth and joy. A different kind of joy. The kind that existed in the spaces between stress and routine. The kind that came with people, with camaraderie, with the small, genuine bonds that made the day bearable.

Today was Tina's birthday—a reason, however brief, to pause. Tina wasn't just a colleague. She was a quiet constant in my life, a steady presence in a world where most people drifted in and out. Where others mistook my silences for arrogance or distance, she understood. She never forced conversations. Never demanded explanations. She just… existed beside me. And in return, I did the same for her.

The conference room had been hastily transformed into a makeshift celebration space. Someone had pinned up a few decorations—uneven balloons taped to the walls, a crooked "Happy Birthday" banner hanging above the whiteboard, the remnants of meetings still scribbled in marker behind it. The room was imperfect, thrown together in a hurry, but somehow, it was perfect. It was ours.

A small group had gathered, a mix of genuine excitement and that half-hearted participation that came with office parties. But Tina—she was happy. I watched her as she moved through the room, her laughter light, her smile wide and unguarded. She looked younger today, freer, her usual composed demeanor softened by the warmth of celebration.

I stood at the back, watching her laugh at some joke, her head thrown back, eyes crinkling at the corners. It was rare to see her like this—unguarded, vulnerable, real. I felt a strange swell of pride, as if her joy was somehow my achievement. As if by simply being here, I was part of her happiness. And that was enough.

We sang. Loud, off-key, laughing between verses. Someone threw an arm around my shoulder, swaying exaggeratedly to the song, making me laugh harder. It was ridiculous, it was imperfect, but it was ours.

The cake-cutting was quick, followed by the usual tradition—smearing icing on the birthday girl's face. Tina groaned dramatically as a swipe of chocolate landed on her cheek, but her laughter rang out, genuine and full.

"Okay, okay, enough!" she scolded, wiping at her face. "Before this turns into a full-fledged food fight!"

I watched as my colleagues bantered, tossing jokes and crumbs at each other, the usual tensions of work momentarily forgotten. I was happy, completely, utterly in the moment.

Tina caught my eye through the chaos, her gaze steady, her smile knowing. She raised an eyebrow as if to say, See? You needed this. And maybe I did.

Maybe, in the middle of overwhelming responsibilities and emotions I still didn't know how to handle, this was exactly what I needed. A pocket of warmth. A moment of lightness. A reminder that I wasn't alone.

It was Tina who made me feel that way. Not by asking questions or giving speeches or offering advice. Just by being there. By being herself. By standing beside me in silence, in laughter, in everything in between.

When the party wound down and people drifted back to their desks, I stayed behind with Tina, the two of us sitting quietly amid the fading signs of celebration—balloons drooping, crumbs scattered, paper plates stacked in surrender.

She nudged me, her smile soft. "You okay?"

I nodded, a warmth spreading through my chest. "Yeah. I am."

And for once, I meant it.

Because no matter how heavy the day felt, no matter how many times I laughed too loud or talked too much, no matter how hollow the silences echoed when the noise faded—Tina was my constant. A steady presence. A quiet understanding. A friendship that didn't need words.

And in a world full of fleeting connections, that was everything.

When the office finally emptied and the fluorescent lights dimmed, I lingered for a moment longer, letting the silence seep in. Then I slipped into my car, closing the door behind me, sealing myself off from the world.

The quiet settled around me, heavy but not unwelcome. I took a deep breath, fingers resting on the steering wheel, my chest rising and falling in slow, deliberate rhythms. I reached over, turned the key, and the engine hummed to life. With a press of a button, the radio filled the car with soft, familiar melodies.

Music had always been my refuge. The place where words turned into emotions, where the world outside could be drowned out by a melody that understood me better than most people ever could. I scrolled through my playlist, landing on a classic Bollywood mix that never failed to lift my spirits. As the opening chords of Arijit Singh played, a smile tugged at my lips.

I pulled out of the parking lot, the city lights stretching out before me like a path lined with tiny, glittering promises. Driving was my escape. My one true escape. It was the place where I could let my mind wander, where I could sing at the top of my lungs without worrying if I was too much. Where the world shrank to just me, the road, and the music. The solitude I had made my own.

Home wasn't a burden—but it wasn't quite a sanctuary either. I liked being there. It was warm in the way only a lived-in space could be. But over the years, it had become a web of routines—roles I knew by heart, needs I could anticipate without a word, tasks that started before I even stepped through the door.

And somewhere in the middle of all that, I'd begun to fade into the background of my own life. Not entirely. Just enough to forget what I liked, what I missed, what made me feel like *me*. It wasn't intentional—it never is.

You tend to the people you love, and little by little, you forget to tend to yourself.

That's why those 45 minutes in the car meant something. The drive home was a soft landing—a buffer between the outside world and the one waiting inside. Music playing, the sky changing color as I moved through traffic. I still had a good two hours before the house came alive again with dinner, questions, and the clatter of everyday life. That window was mine. Not loud, not grand, but wholly mine. Just enough space to remember who I was before stepping back into who I needed to be.

I kicked off my heels, feeling the tension in my shoulders ease as I sank into my recliner, the familiarity of the space grounding me. A cup of black coffee in hand— my quiet rebellion against the world's relentless demands. No unnecessary conversations. No urgent messages. Just the faint hum of the refrigerator and the soft ticking of the clock on the wall.

This was my breathing space. Not a sanctuary, not quite. But a small stretch of time where I didn't have to perform. Where I could loosen the grip, drop the roles, and just exist. Even when the silence felt too sharp, even when the stillness reminded me of everything I wasn't saying—I held onto it. This quiet hour was mine. A moment untouched by anyone else's needs.

Just the flicker of Netflix against the walls, casting moving shadows of love stories across a life that never quite resembled one. I watched absently as romance unfolded in its usual arcs—hearts colliding, souls aligning, promises whispered in dim lighting. They fell in love so easily, so inevitably, as if fate had drawn their names in cursive across the sky.

I never really believed in that kind of love—the breathless kind, the aching kind. For me, love had always been steady. Practical. It meant showing up, choosing each other, doing the hard things even when you didn't feel like it. And yes, that *is* love. A quiet, unwavering kind. The kind that stays.

But somewhere beneath all that steadiness lived a quieter truth. A flicker I couldn't quite extinguish. I wanted more. I wanted to be wanted—not out of habit, not out of duty, but out of desire. I wanted to be kissed with intention, to feel the heat of someone's gaze settle on me like fire. To feel the butterflies, the spark, the kind of love that made my chest tighten and my breath catch. The kind that made the air feel different. The kind that whispered magic into the mundane. Not a responsibility, but a choice—a wild, deliberate, heart-racing choice.

The movie droned on—laughter in the rain, slow dances under string lights, declarations that made even silence feel poetic. It was the same story I'd seen a hundred times, and yet… I kept watching. Because maybe, deep down, I still wanted to believe in that kind of magic. In the idea that love could be something more.

A hopeless romantic? Maybe. Not that anyone would know. I was the strong one. The one with the answers, the cheer, the stories that made people laugh. The one who held others up, who never let her cracks show. I had perfected the art of being fine.

But in the stillness of my own space, with nothing but flickering light and shadows for company, the mask loosened. Loneliness crept in—familiar, quiet, not loud enough to break me, just enough to make itself known.

I watched them kiss on-screen, their words full of fire and softness, of need and recognition. And I told myself I didn't need that. I was strong. Independent. Whole. I didn't need saving. I didn't need anyone to complete me.

But the truth? I wanted it.

Not perfection. Not roses and candlelit clichés. Just something *real*. Something raw. Something that saw through my smiles and right into the silences. A love that made me feel heard, made me feel wanted, made me feel *alive*. A presence that softened the quiet, that stayed when the laughter faded.

The credits rolled. The room dimmed. I didn't press play on another film. I just sat there, surrounded by the hum of evening and the weight of everything that still needed to be done—dinner, laundry, the mess in the kitchen, the people who would soon fill the space again.

But I lingered.

Because maybe, somewhere in the ordinary, I was still waiting. Maybe beneath the checklists and the roles, I was still holding space for a story of my own.

Because even now, in the quiet, in the flickering shadows… I still believed in the possibility of magic.

THE DISTRACTION THAT ALWAYS CAME KNOCKING

The shrill ring of my phone cut through the stillness.

"Urmi."

I sighed, letting the exhaustion settle in my voice as I answered. "Hello."

Urmi was a force of nature—unapologetic, wild, untethered in a way I both admired and resisted. She moved like the world was hers to play with, like hesitation was a language she never learned. And yet, beneath that fire, there were moments—fleeting, quiet—where I saw a mind just as restless as mine. That's what made our friendship feel oddly effortless. We never sat down to unravel our emotions or search for meaning. We existed in parallel—through music, through dance, through nights that felt like escapes from the heaviness neither of us wanted to name. We were similar in ways we never spoke about, different in ways we never tried to fix. Chaos met calm, instinct met thought. And somewhere in that collision, we found rhythm.

There was no pressure to be vulnerable, no expectations to bare our souls. Just rhythm, laughter, and the understanding that sometimes, life needed to be drowned out. And in that moment, as I listened to her voice fill the quiet I had just created,

I wondered— Was I really unwinding in my solitude? Or was I just hiding from everything I didn't want to feel?

'What's with the gloom?' Her energy buzzed through the receiver. 'Let's meet for tea.'

I frowned. 'You know I don't drink tea.'

"I know. But I do. And I miss you." Her tone was playful, laced with a mischief that always made me wary. "Also… Yash agreed to meet. Come with me? I don't want to go alone."

Yash.

A name that had lingered at the edges of our conversations. Someone she had noticed long before I ever paid him any attention. Handsome. Intriguing. I'd spoken to him maybe twice—just enough to remember the timbre of his voice—and exchanged a few casual messages over time. Brief, passing conversations that barely skimmed the surface. Nothing deep, nothing memorable. I'd told myself it was nothing—just light, forgettable chatter.

And yet, somehow, he'd stayed. Quietly lodged in the back of my mind.

There was no logical reason for my curiosity. No story, no history, nothing to hold onto. Just a name that echoed longer than it should have, carrying a weight I couldn't explain. He wasn't a fantasy. Not even a crush. Just a quiet pull. The kind that sneaks in unnoticed and refuses to leave.

I didn't know why he always made my heart beat a little faster. But he did.

"I'm drained, Urmi. I just want to rest."

She laughed on the other end of the line, her voice bubbling with that familiar mix of charm and persistence.

"Oh, come on," she coaxed. "You'll have fun. You're good at conversations—you can talk to anyone and everyone. You're always the light at every party."

There was a pause—long enough to feel deliberate, like a dare.

And yet, for all that fire, first meetings made her nervous—though she'd never admit it outright. That's probably why she wanted me to come along. Moral support, she'd said.

"I'll do all the talking anyway," she added, a smirk practically audible. "You just sit there and pretend to listen. You're good at that too."

I rolled my eyes, fingers tightening around the phone. She was relentless. Still mid-persuasion, her voice playful and insistent—

And then another call lit up my screen.

Yash.

My breath hitched.

His name glowed across the screen, bold and unexpected, demanding my attention.

"What is it?" Urmi asked, her tone turning sly, her curiosity sharp.

"It's Yash," I said quietly, my heart doing an involuntary flip.

"Pick up and say yes," she ordered, her voice thick with mischief.

As my thumb hovered over the green button, I hesitated. My heart pounded in a way that felt both ridiculous and impossible to ignore. I didn't really know him—not beyond those fleeting words and second-hand impressions. He was just a name. Just a face.

And yet… something in me kept circling back to him.

I answered, my voice cautious, composed.

"Hello."

His voice was smooth, familiar, and frustratingly effortless, as if the entire day hadn't drained him the way it had drained me. 'Free or caught in the whirlwind of the day?'

'Free, but exhausted,' I muttered, rubbing my temples.

Yash: Tea?

I leaned back, my fingers absentmindedly tracing the edge of my phone, my shoulders relaxing just a little. I was tired. Exhausted, really. But suddenly, the thought of going out didn't feel so heavy. Suddenly, the idea of meeting him didn't seem so exhausting.

Feel like a change of scenery?"

I hesitated, my mind already forming excuses, already building walls. But for some reason, the words wouldn't come. I found myself wanting to hear more. Wanting to see if his presence was as easy as his voice. Wanting to satisfy a curiosity I didn't know I had.

"I don't know," I said finally, my voice softer, unsure. "I was planning on just staying in tonight."

"That sounds nice," he replied, his words genuine, unforced. "But so does tea with good company."

A laugh escaped me. 'Not a tea person. After today, I'd rather have a beer.'

Instead of hesitation, he surprised me. 'Fine. Beer it is.'

I felt a smile creep onto my face, a warmth spreading through my chest. He wasn't trying to convince me. He wasn't pushing. He was just... there. Present. Uncomplicated.

And for some reason, I wanted to know more. I wanted to see if his presence could make the quiet feel less heavy. I wanted to understand why his voice made me feel this way. I stared at my reflection in the dark screen of my TV, caught between intrigue and reluctance.

'I'm too tired to dress up, let alone drive anywhere.' His response was immediate. 'Then don't. He cut in, his tone calm but resolute. I'll pick you up. Stay in your pajamas if you want- he added, like it was the most obvious thing in the world. —be comfortable.'

A slow frown crept onto my face. Was he serious?

I hesitated, letting the silence stretch for a moment, expecting him to add something—maybe a joke, maybe a tease. But he didn't. He meant it.

"Send me your location," he said after a pause. "I'm leaving the office now."

My fingers hovered over the screen, uncertainty curling in my chest. Why was I hesitating?

"It's out of your way," I pointed out, knowing full well that wasn't the real reason for my hesitation.

"I want to." His response was immediate, unwavering.

A small exhale left my lips, my stomach twisting with something that wasn't quite nervousness, but wasn't entirely calm either.

"Just wait for my call," he added.

There was no question in his voice. It wasn't a request. It was a certainty. And then he hung up.

I bit my lip, staring at the text box in front of me. Was I really going to do this? I could say no. I could tell him I was too tired. That I had work in the morning. That I just wanted a quiet night to myself. But did I? Because the truth was, I liked the way he said it. Not asking, not doubting—just knowing.

Like I was something worth the effort. And that… that did something to me. I typed my location and hit send. A minute later, his response came. "See you soon."

I slipped the phone into my pocket, my heart still fluttering in that stupid, ridiculous way I didn't want to admit felt good. There was no reason for it—a voice that had caught me off guard, a flicker of curiosity I hadn't realized was there, a distraction that, for once, felt oddly welcome.

His certainty rattled me. Why was I agreeing so easily? When Urmi had asked, I had every excuse ready. But now? I wasn't even pretending to hesitate. Something about him—his voice, his presence—pulled me in. And for the first time in a long time, I didn't want to resist. I wanted to go.

The night stretched before me, crisp and humming with an unspoken electricity, pulsing with possibilities, yet inside my apartment, the air felt different—heavy with indecision.

I stood before my wardrobe, fingers skimming through choices, my mind trapped in a battle I couldn't quite rationalize, slipping between textures as if the answer could be found in the folds of a dress or the comfort of an old sweater. The simplest decision—what to wear—felt like a choice far bigger than it should have been.

Dress up or dress down? If I dressed up, would it seem like I was trying too hard? Would it send the wrong message? Would it send the right one?

If I kept it casual, would I regret not making an effort? Would he even notice? Would I want him to?

My eyes landed on the sleek black dress hanging neatly in the corner. Bold. Confident. A statement. But was I ready to make one? My hands shifted to my well-worn hoodie—the safe choice, the one that never demanded too much from me. It would be easier—to keep it simple, to remain unfazed. But something inside me itched at the idea of playing it safe.

A floral-strapped top—delicate, feminine, yet casual. Soft fabric with tiny printed blossoms, subtle enough not to overwhelm, yet charming in a way I couldn't quite explain. The kind of top that made me feel beautiful without trying too hard. The kind that felt like just enough.

I pulled it over my head, the straps resting lightly against my shoulders, exposing just a hint of skin. Not too much. Not too little.

Then came my favorite blue jeans—the ones that hugged me just right, slightly faded at the knees, lived-in, comfortable. The kind of jeans that had been through late-night drives, spontaneous coffee dates, long walks under streetlights, and quiet moments that didn't need words.

I looked in the mirror. It wasn't glamorous. It wasn't extravagant. But it was me. And yet, as I stood there, fingers tugging at the hem instinctively, I felt that creeping uncertainty slither back in.

Was it too much? Too little? Too revealing? A moment of doubt flickered in my mind, a reflex I hadn't quite shaken off over the years. Why did it even matter?

But then, I thought of Yash. Of how he had told me to be comfortable. Of how he hadn't asked for effort, just for presence. And that was what I was giving him—me, exactly as I was.

I grabbed a white sweater, wrapping it around me like armor, letting its warmth ground me, offering a quiet reassurance against the flicker of unease. Beyond my window, the December night stretched out, wild and waiting, the wind howling through the trees, carrying the kind of anticipation that came before something unknown.

And yet, despite the winter chill, my skin felt warm. Not from the sweater. But from the awareness thrumming beneath it. Because I knew what I was doing. This wasn't just a meeting. And yet, I was still pretending it was.

The version of Yash I had was the one Urmi had painted for me- Her excitement, her lingering mentions of him, the way she had noticed him. Her words had built him in my mind long before I had even spoken to him—a man of quiet confidence, of presence. A man whose name surfaced in our conversations more often than she realized.

Yash was handsome, younger, straightforward to the point of being almost blunt. A man who spoke his mind without hesitation or overthinking—a trait that felt almost foreign to me. And yet, here I was. Dressing up for a man I barely knew. Even though I had every reason not to. Even though he was supposed to be Urmi's crush.

But I couldn't forget the sight of her that night, the call that changed everything— Sitting next to Yash, drink in hand, her laughter spilling through the screen like an afterthought.

That night, 11th of September, my phone had lit up unexpectedly with a video call from Urmi. I hesitated before answering.

"Urmi?" I said, confused. My voice had held the usual warmth, the ease of friendship. But I wasn't prepared for what I saw. The screen flickered, and there she was— flushed cheeks, slightly messy hair, her voice dripping with excitement. Behind her, the dim glow of a place I didn't recognize.

And then... Yash.

I blinked.

"Guess where I am?" she teased, giggling.

She turned the camera briefly, giving me a dizzying glimpse of him. Sitting casually. Drink in hand. His posture relaxed, with that quiet kind of ease people don't learn—they just have. He didn't speak. Didn't even look at the camera right away.

But Urmi? She was glowing. Her laughter spilled through the screen, unfiltered, unguarded, as if she had already forgotten I was watching. As if she was living in a moment that I wasn't supposed to be part of.

I forced a polite smile, muttered a quick "Hi, hello", and ended the call within a minute. I wasn't interested. I didn't know him. And, frankly, I didn't understand why she wanted me to be part of this moment. The next day, Urmi called me, her voice unusually subdued.

"The Gin didn't suit me," she admitted. "I felt sick. Had to rush back to my apartment."

"You left?" I asked.

"Yeah," she sighed. "I left my handbag at his place in all the rush. Had to go back the next morning to get it."

That's when she told me what had really bothered her. "When I went to collect it… he barely looked at me," she said quietly. "Just handed me the bag and that was it." There was a pause. Then, softer—"I felt so embarrassed."

She had wanted the night to continue with him. Even though nothing had happened between them, she had imagined something more. But when she saw him the next day, when he barely acknowledged her, the feeling of rejection hit harder than she expected.

I had tried to brush it off for her sake. "Maybe you're overthinking. If you really like him, why don't you invite him for a cup of tea?"

She let out a humorless laugh. "Bad idea. I'll just let the feeling pass on its own."

That was supposed to be the end of it. Yash was her story. Her unfinished sentence. Not mine.

Urmi had been noticing Yash long before that night. She used to mention how she would catch glimpses of him from her window when he left for work in the mornings. Then, during one of our usual calls, when I casually mentioned I was looking for a job change, she immediately suggested— "Maybe Yash can guide you."

Before I could even process the idea, she had already passed me his number. I had shrugged it off at the time, noncommittal.

"Let's see. I might call him tomorrow." But I never did.

Days turned into weeks, and Yash remained nothing more than a name in my phone. A number I had no intention of dialing.

And then, on the 26th of October, late in the evening, my phone buzzed with an unexpected message. It was only a message. One that should've faded like the rest. But it stayed with me, quietly, stubbornly.

"Hey! Got your number from Urmi."

I hadn't even seen his message that night. The next morning, when I finally noticed it, I replied— "Ya, Urmi gave me your number too. Was thinking of messaging you today."

His reply came almost immediately. "Call?"

Before I knew it, I was on a call with him. It wasn't flirty. It wasn't deep. Just a casual conversation about career, workplaces, random things. It wasn't supposed to mean anything. But somehow, it did.

THE UNSPOKEN SHIFT

The next day, in between sips of coffee, I found myself mentioning it to Tina. Without meaning to. Without realizing how easily it had slipped into my thoughts. "I don't know why, but I actually enjoyed talking to him," I admitted, half-smiling, almost as if I were testing the thought out loud.

Tina's reaction was instant— Eyes wide with mischief, a smirk playing on her lips. "Oh? That's new. You don't usually entertain random conversations."

"I know," I said, almost to myself. "But it was… nice. Just a casual chat, nothing serious."

"Nothing serious," she repeated, drawing out the words, eyeing me like she didn't believe a word I was saying.

Then her smirk grew wider. "Oh my god, you're smiling while talking about him. Look at you!"

I rolled my eyes. "Shut up, Tina."

But she wasn't letting go. And neither was I. Because somewhere in all of this, something had shifted. Something I wasn't ready to admit.

Tina was relentless. Over the next few days, she teased me every time she caught that fleeting smile on my face—the one I hadn't even realized I was wearing.

"Is that Yash messaging you?" she would ask, her eyebrow arching with knowing amusement. I brushed it off. Every single time. "God, Tina, it's nothing."

"Mhm. Sure. You're just grinning at your phone for no reason?"

"It's just casual conversations." And it was. Or at least, it should have been.

There was nothing suggestive in Yash's messages— just a quiet sincerity that stayed with me. They didn't carry hidden meaning or hint at anything more. If anything, they were practical—maybe once, just to check in. Maybe twice, when he'd asked for my resume, mentioning he knew someone who could help with job opportunities. Simple. Straightforward. Nothing that should have lingered longer than a moment.

I never sent it. Not because I didn't want to, but because life got in the way. My mother had fallen ill, and my world had shrunk overnight—hospital visits, medications, doctor calls, and the kind of exhaustion that settles deep into your bones and makes even the simplest tasks feel impossible.

He had followed up. Once. Twice. I never got around to it. But I always replied. Even if it was just a short text. Even if I told myself it didn't mean anything.

And yet, somehow, it did. Seeing his name light up on my screen made me pause, even on the heaviest days. Made something in me shift—subtle, quiet, but undeniable. Like a weight I hadn't noticed I was carrying had momentarily eased. It was strange, how something so small could do that. How a message with no expectation behind it could settle into the quiet spaces I'd long since stopped sharing with anyone.

It wasn't anything, I reminded myself. It wasn't meant to be. But it still felt like someone had noticed. Like someone, even in passing, had thought of me. And wasn't that a dangerous thing to get used to? I wasn't supposed to feel this way. I had spent years learning not to expect much. Years training myself to be fine on my own, to manage without leaning. But Yash had a way of slipping through the cracks. He wasn't charming in the way people usually notice. There was no effort to impress, no polished lines or cleverness. He was calm, grounded— like gravity in human form. The kind of presence that didn't demand space, but drew you in anyway.

And somehow, that made all the difference.

And yet, here I was. Now, standing in front of my wardrobe, I felt that weight again. What was I doing? Why was I meeting him? I had every reason not to. And yet, despite the logic, despite my own rules, I hadn't said no.

I exhaled, tugging the sweater tighter around my body like a shield. It was too late to back out now. I reached for my perfume, letting the familiar scent settle over me—a quiet reassurance, a reminder that I was still in control. I traced a soft line of eyeliner along my eyes, just enough to make them look fresh, more awake. A swipe of nude lipstick—subtle, understated. Just enough to feel put together.

And yet, beneath the carefully assembled exterior, something felt off-balance. Something in me knew— I was standing at the edge of something I couldn't quite define.

I was contradictions woven together—an extrovert who craved silences, a woman who could hold a room yet struggled to hold her own emotions, someone who had always been surrounded by people, conversations, stories—the effortless exchange of words, the way connections sparked through shared laughter, through knowing glances- but never quite let anyone in.

I thrived in the noise, in the rush of interactions, in the warmth of company. But I also loved my silences. The quiet moments where the world felt distant, where I could exist without performing, without being anyone but myself. I was the type to fill a room and disappear in the same breath—engaged, yet always slightly elsewhere. And maybe that was the problem. Maybe that was why I felt this constant pull—toward people, toward love, yet always hesitant, always stepping back before I could fall too deep.

The hardest thing had always been understanding myself, I had spent years trying to figure myself out. And failing. The truth was, I was careful. Careful with love. Careful with trust. Careful with myself. And yet, here I was, waiting for Yash to arrive.

My thoughts twisted into familiar knots, like a war inside my head, looping back to the same questions I had been asking myself all evening. Why didn't I say no? Why was I here? Why did I care so much about how I looked tonight?

Excuses lingered at the edges of my mind, lined up in perfect reasoning— "You're tired." "This is unnecessary." "Urmi saw him first." "You don't even know him."

But none of them were loud enough to change the fact that I was here. That I had chosen to be.

My phone buzzed in my hand.

Yash. - "Five more minutes, and I'll be there. Will you come down?"

His voice was smooth, calm—like he already knew my answer.

I exhaled slowly, my fingers hovering over the screen for a second longer than necessary before I replied.

"Yes."

Stepping outside, I stood near my gate, my breath curling into the cold air. The December night was biting, creeping under my sweater, wrapping around my skin like a whispered warning. My fingers instinctively curled into the fabric, as if holding onto something familiar would steady the unraveling inside me.

Somewhere deep down, I expected to see Urmi in the car. Maybe because her presence would make this easier—make it feel less like something new, less like something I was stepping into alone.

If it weren't for her, I wouldn't have even known him. She saw him first, laughed about his quirks, dissected every word and pause like they meant something. Maybe they did. Maybe in another life, he was meant to be hers—and I had no business stepping in. But that wasn't this reality. Because when Yash's car pulled up, his headlights slicing through the dimly lit street, there was no Urmi. Just him. Just me. And suddenly, a slow awareness settled over me. This wasn't about her anymore.

He didn't get out. Didn't text to say he was there.

He just leaned over and pushed the door open, smooth and unthinking—like he already knew I'd hesitate. It was nothing, really. Just a gesture. But it caught on something soft in me, something I thought I'd long buried. No words passed between us. No promises. Just a pause. A door open. A decision waiting. And all I could hear was the sound of my own wanting, loud in the silence.

I hesitated—just for a fraction of a second. Then, before I could second-guess myself, I slid into the seat, shutting the door behind me. The space inside the car felt smaller than it should have. The air, thicker. The quiet hum of the stereo played low, filling the silence without really drowning it.

"Hi," he said, turning his head slightly, his voice softer than I expected. Casual. Unrushed. But carrying a weight I couldn't quite place. "We finally meet."

"Yes," I murmured. Finally!

And then I made the mistake of looking at him.

Because the moment I did, something shifted. Not in a dreamy, slow-motion, violins-playing kind of way—but in a far more dangerous one. The kind that sneaks up on you and steals your breath before you even realize you're holding it.

He was undeniably hot—the kind of man who didn't have to try. That scruffy beard, the chiseled jaw, the quiet confidence in the way he sat like the world didn't touch him. He wasn't loud or flashy. He didn't need to be. His presence filled the space in a way that made everything else blur at the edges.

And yes—I was the one staring. Silently. Shamelessly. I couldn't help myself.

I'd seen attractive men before. Admired them. Laughed with them, flirted maybe. But none of them had ever made me feel this.

This pull.

A slow, electric hum beneath my skin that made me forget how to sit still.

Then—his eyes.

He had only looked at me once. Just once. A glance, really. But it was enough to ruin me.

Dark. Deep. Not just intense, but penetrating. The kind of eyes that didn't flirt—they stripped. Like they were made of fire and shadow. There was heat in them, yes, but also a kind of knowing. Like they had lived through things. Like they had carried things. And just for that brief second, they landed on me—steady, unwavering— and I forgot how to be composed.

And then… he looked away.

I should have looked away too. I didn't.

My gaze lingered on him like I was studying a painting, trying to memorize every line, every flicker of emotion that crossed his face. And then—he looked back. Just a flick of the eyes. But maybe… maybe he realized.

Maybe he saw me staring.

Oh god.

My stomach dropped. My pulse thudded in my throat.

What if he knew?

What if he could feel the heat building inside me?

Why was I behaving like this?

I wasn't a teenager. I wasn't the kind to melt under a glance. And yet here I was—heart racing, thoughts spinning, terrified that he could read the desire written all over my face.

I needed to stop.

Now.

Before he saw it all—the flutter in my chest, the breath that caught in my throat, the silent, aching way I was already leaning toward him.

And then, without warning, another sense betrayed me—his scent.

God.

Cedarwood. Musk. Earthy, warm, and something else I couldn't name. Expensive but understated, like everything else about him. It didn't shout—it lingered. It curled through the air between us, pulling me in with every inhale. It was subtle, masculine, and wildly distracting.

Like him, it felt familiar and unfamiliar all at once. And it made my head spin in the best, most dangerous way.

Without even realizing it, something inside me tilted. My body didn't move, but I felt it—like an invisible shift. A surrender I hadn't agreed to but didn't resist.

This wasn't just physical.

This wasn't flirtation.

This was awareness.

This was desire wrapped in stillness, in silence, in every glance I tried not to hold.

And I didn't know if I wanted to feed it or run from it.

Urmi's call shattered the silence, jolting me from the web of thoughts that had tangled inside my head.

Urmi: Where are you?

Me: Five minutes away

Yash, who had been driving with the kind of ease that came from instinct, took a quick glance at the screen before turning the car towards the metro station to pick her up. In a blink, it changed, and an uneasy weight settled in my chest. I shouldn't be here.

The thought crept in before I could stop it.

It wasn't like Yash and I had anything—not really. Just a few messages. A call. A meeting that wasn't even planned. And yet, something about tonight felt like a line I wasn't sure I should be near.

And now, I was here. In his car. Sitting beside him.

Was I imagining it? Overthinking?

Or was this something I shouldn't want—but did anyway?

The headlights of approaching cars streaked past, illuminating the dashboard in brief flashes. I caught a glimpse of my reflection in the window—my lips pressed together, my expression unreadable.

Was I overthinking? Maybe. But the feeling wouldn't leave me. And then—we arrived.

She slid into the back seat, her usual brightness intact—smooth, instinctive. But I caught it. That flicker-the flicker in her eyes. That quick, barely-there look in her eyes. Disappointment. She had expected the front seat. Her seat. It was subtle. Almost nothing.

Almost. But I saw it before she buried it beneath a light-hearted comment, filling the space between us with words, as if that fleeting moment had never existed.

And I wondered—was I imagining things? Or did she already know?

Urmi launched into conversation—casual, breezy, like she always did.

But I felt his presence beside me. Felt the way his gaze flicked toward me every now and then—quick, almost unnoticeable, but deliberate. Like he was checking if I was okay. Like he was making sure I was still with him, still in this moment.

And every time I felt the weight of his eyes on me, I couldn't ignore the pull between us. Something was shifting. Something unspoken, undeniable, irreversible. And the worst part? Urmi felt it too.

"Where to?" Yash's voice was steady, unaffected. Like the silence before it hadn't existed.

"Let's go to ZEE." I muttered

He nodded, his grip shifting on the steering wheel as he eased into traffic. Bangalore's roads pulsed around us—an unending river of frustration, honking cars, impatient drivers. But Yash navigated through it like it didn't touch him.

His fingers moved with practiced ease—gripping, releasing, shifting gears with the kind of control that made everything else seem secondary. There was something undeniably captivating about the way certain men drove—controlled, unbothered, like the chaos outside couldn't touch them. Like nothing could. It was hypnotic in a way I didn't want to admit.

And yet, my mind wasn't in the car. It was somewhere else—stuck in a loop, replaying the look in Urmi's eyes. That fleeting flicker. The way she masked it too quickly. The way she didn't say a word about where I was sitting. Maybe it didn't mean anything. Or maybe it meant everything.

"How long to reach?" Urmi asked, leaning forward slightly, her voice carrying a mix of impatience and anticipation.

Yash, his eyes still steady on the road, glanced at the map on his phone before responding. "Fifteen more minutes." His voice was calm, steady, as if urgency had no place around him.

Urmi exhaled dramatically, slumping back into her seat. "Ugh, Bangalore traffic. This city is a mess."

I chuckled, my fingers idly tracing patterns on my jeans. "You say this like it's new. We've been suffering for years."

Yash smirked, the corners of his lips tugging just slightly. "She just likes to complain," he said, casting a quick glance at Urmi through the rearview mirror.

Urmi rolled her eyes. "I have the right to! I could've been home by now, in my PJs, binge-watching Netflix."

Yash shook his head, adjusting his grip on the steering wheel. "No one begged you to come."

She gasped, feigning betrayal. "Excuse me? I was the one who asked you to meet, remember?"

He exhaled, a smile playing on his lips. "Exactly. You dragged me into this."

"And you're lucky I did," she shot back. "Admit it—you'd have just sulked at home with your headphones on."

I watched the exchange in silence, a small smile lingering on my lips. Fifteen more minutes. It wasn't long, but it was enough. Enough time to steal glances at Yash when he wasn't looking. Enough time to notice how his fingers tapped lightly against the steering wheel, keeping time with the faint music playing through the car speakers. Enough time to realize how naturally we all fit into this moment, and yet—how something had started to shift.

Urmi and Yash. Yash and me. Me and Urmi. A dynamic that had once been simple wasn't so simple anymore.

Fifteen minutes wasn't long. But it was long enough to realize that something between us was quietly, irreversibly changing

A TANGLE OF EMOTIONS

ZEE wasn't just another restaurant—it was my place, my oasis. A quiet retreat tucked away in the heart of the city, where the noise and chaos of the outside world seemed to vanish as soon as I stepped through the door. It was my little sanctuary, where for a few precious hours, I didn't have to carry the weight of the day, didn't have to be anything but a woman unwinding, letting go of all the burdens I had been carrying.

I had been coming here long before this night, long before Yash was anything more than a name in Urmi's stories.

Tina and I had spent countless evenings here after work, tucked into a corner table with beers in hand, shaking off the exhaustion of long days and longer expectations. It was our reset button. A place where we could throw our worries onto the table, sip them away, and remind ourselves that life was more than just deadlines and responsibilities.

So when I suggested ZEE that night, it was second nature. I hadn't thought twice about it.

But as we walked in, the moment stretched just a little too long. The hostess saw me, and her face lit up with recognition.

"Welcome back!" she said warmly, like she always did. And then she looked at Yash.

Something flickered across her face—not surprise, but something close.

I caught it. A silent acknowledgment, a glance that said she had seen me here before, but not with him. For a brief moment, I wondered what it looked like from the outside. A woman—composed, familiar—walking in with a younger man who wasn't just anyone.

I smiled, brushing off the thought.

"No reservation?" she asked, already knowing the answer.

"Not today," I replied. "A table for three—rooftop preferred."

She led us up a narrow, winding staircase, her footsteps light yet deliberate, as if she had taken this path a thousand times before. The air grew thinner with each step, anticipation building within me. At the top, she paused for just a moment before pressing her palm against the heavy door. With a gentle push, it creaked open, unveiling the rooftop bathed in the golden embrace of the setting sun.

A soft breeze curled around us, carrying with it the scent of the city—faint traces of street food, distant laughter, and something unmistakably electric, as if the night itself was coming alive. As we stepped onto the open space, the world seemed to expand. The city stretched endlessly before us, a glittering labyrinth of flickering lights and shifting shadows, each window and streetlamp holding a story of its own.

The rooftop buzzed with quiet energy—a hum of conversation, the clinking of glasses, the occasional burst of laughter that drifted into the night. The air was crisp, cool against my skin, laced with a kind of familiarity that should have been comforting. It always had been before. And yet, tonight, something felt different. The warmth of nostalgia lingered just beyond my reach, teasing but never quite settling. But tonight, something felt different.

I settled into my seat, watching as Yash and Urmi did the same.

We were talking—or at least, I was. Filling the space as I always did, letting words spill out without pause. Urmi, on the other hand, sat stiffly, her usual ease absent, her words measured. And Yash—he was just listening, eyes flicking between us, absorbing more than he let on.

This was my place. My familiar haven, my usual escape. But tonight, it felt foreign, as if the air had shifted in some imperceptible way, leaving me untethered, out of sync with the rhythm I once knew.

The beer arrived, followed by snacks, clinking glasses, and talk that rose and fell like an old, familiar song. It should have felt natural. It always did with Urmi around. She had a way of keeping the energy alive, filling the air so seamlessly that silence never had the chance to settle.

But I felt it. Even as I laughed at something she said, even as I took slow sips of my drink, there was a part of me that wasn't fully here. A part of me that was watching, standing at the edge of it all, waiting to understand why tonight felt different.

"Got cigarettes?" Yash asked, turning to Urmi.

She nodded without hesitation. "In my bag."

And then it happened. Before I could register the shift, Yash reached over—unzipping her bag, his fingers moving through her things without a second thought. It was seamless. Practiced. Familiar. Too familiar.

Urmi didn't even blink. Didn't react. She kept talking, kept sipping her beer, as if this was nothing.

And that was what unsettled me the most—not what he did, but how instinctively it came to him. How unquestioningly she let it happen. There was no hesitation. No second glance. No awareness that there was another set of eyes watching. Because this wasn't new, maybe this was routine.

I reached for my glass, my fingers curling around the cool condensation. It was grounding, but not enough. Something had shifted in the air, something that pressed against my chest, heavy and unshakable.

I didn't like it. Not the way it felt. Not the way it made me second-guess myself. Was I overanalysing? Was this just my mind playing tricks on me? Or was I seeing something I wasn't meant to see?

Yash lit his cigarette. The ember flared briefly before settling into a slow burn, the glow casting fleeting shadows across his face. He exhaled, his lips curving slightly around the movement—unbothered, at ease, completely in his element.

Smoke curled around me, thick and intrusive, pressing into my skin, my hair, my lungs. I hated it. I always had. But tonight, the discomfort ran deeper.

Urmi lit hers, too. The flick of her lighter was smooth, practiced. A ritual. She passed it over without looking, their fingers brushing—fleeting, insignificant. Or maybe it wasn't. Maybe it was everything.

I looked away. But not before I saw it.

Yash—watching me. Not directly, just a flicker from the corner of his eye. Subtle. Barely there. But there. Like he was reading me. Like he could see the thoughts unraveling in real-time, tracing the shape of something unspoken. And for the first time that night, I didn't know how to hold that gaze. Didn't know what to do with the weight of being seen.

Then, without warning, the moment shifted. Slipped away like smoke.

A question, light and casual. A harmless, passing thing. "Where is your hometown?"

People ask that all the time, without thinking. Just something to keep the conversation going, something to fill the spaces between sips of beer and flicks of cigarette ash.

But with Yash, it wasn't just a question. His voice carried something different. A weight. A slow, deliberate interest that settled into the air between us. Like he wasn't just making conversation. Like he actually wanted to know. Like my answer mattered.

I hesitated. Not because I didn't want to answer, but because I suddenly felt too aware of him. Of his gaze, the quiet intensity in his presence.

"I'm from—" I gave him just the name. Nothing else. That should have been the end of it. But it wasn't.

Because he listened. Really listened. Not with half his mind somewhere else, the way most people do. Not with polite nods and absent-minded hums.

No! - His attention locked onto me, unwavering. Like he was pulling something out of me, word by word. Like every sentence I spoke was another puzzle piece sliding into place. And before I knew it, I was saying more than I had intended. Memories slipping out between casual sentences. Details I hadn't planned to share.

And then—"Wait… you're from there too?" The realization cracked open the air between us. Something shifted. A thin, electric thread wove itself between us, subtle but impossible to ignore. Recognition. Familiarity. A connection we hadn't expected. A connection I didn't want to feel, but did.

Urmi.

She had been there a second ago. Filling the space with laughter, nudging me, throwing playful glances my way, teasing in a way that made everything feel light.

But now? Now, she wasn't laughing. The warmth in her expression had dimmed, her smile still in place—but barely. It was tight. Stretched. A little too controlled. She wasn't saying anything, but I saw it.

The flicker of something—hurt? disappointment? something else?—before she forced herself to sip her drink. Before she tucked a strand of hair behind her ear in a way that felt too precise. A mask slipping into place. I hadn't done anything wrong. And yet, it felt like I had. There was no guilt inside me. I wanted this. I was almost sure I wanted this moment to continue.

Yash hadn't moved closer. He hadn't said anything inappropriate. And yet, the air between us had changed. Urmi felt it. I felt it.

And Yash? He knew exactly what he was doing.

Even when he turned his gaze back to his drink, even when he exhaled a slow stream of smoke, his focus flicking to me in the quiet way he always did—through the side of his eyes, like he was reading me without words. Possessive. Subtle, but present. Like he had just marked a territory he hadn't even spoken out loud.

"Come to the washroom with me?" The words left my lips too quickly. I wasn't even sure why I said it.

Maybe to break whatever had settled between us. Maybe to give Urmi a moment, to let her know she still belonged in this dynamic.

Or maybe… maybe because I needed to step away. To breathe. To think. To figure out why Yash's presence felt like it was creeping under my skin, wrapping itself around my senses in a way I wasn't prepared for.

Urmi hesitated for a fraction of a second. Then she nodded. And as we stood up, I felt it again—Yash watching me. Not stopping me. Not saying anything. Just watching. Like he already knew I'd come back. Like he wasn't worried about losing my attention. Like he knew exactly where this was heading.

I had to show her. Had to make it look unrehearsed. Like this was just a normal conversation, like I wasn't feeling the weight of her words pressing down on my chest, like I wasn't unravelling at the edges in a way I couldn't afford to show. The escape I needed, but didn't really want.

Urmi couldn't know. She couldn't see that something inside me had already begun to shift. So I smiled. A slow, careful curve of my lips. The kind that was practiced, perfected—a shield I had worn for years, through work meetings, family obligations, and the endless expectations that came with simply existing as a woman who always had to have it together.

And just like that, we left the table behind. But the truth? I knew— The moment the ground shifted, everything I thought was steady suddenly felt uncertain, as if the world beneath me had rearranged itself in a way I couldn't yet understand. Whatever had shifted in the air tonight wasn't something I could just walk away from.

Inside the washroom, the dim lighting cast long, muted shadows across the mirrors, the soft hum of distant music filling the space between us. For a brief second, neither of us spoke. Then, Urmi inhaled, turned to me, and said the words that would lodge themselves into my bones.

"I like him, you know that, right?" Her voice wasn't tentative. It wasn't searching for approval, wasn't waiting for permission. It was matter-of-fact. Like she had already decided how this was going to go. Like this was a truth she had been holding onto, waiting for the right moment to lay bare. Something cold and sharp sliced through the air between us.

I barely had time to process it before she went on.

"But how do I make a move? How do I let him know without being too obvious?" She wasn't asking if she should. She was asking how.

The words landed like a stone in my stomach. Heavy. Unmovable. I swallowed, forcing my breath to stay even, my expression to remain unreadable. But something sharp and unfamiliar pressed against my ribcage, curling itself into my chest with a quiet, insistent ache.

I met her gaze, searching—for hesitation, for doubt, for some flicker of uncertainty that I could latch onto. A loophole. A way out. But all I found was certainty. She wanted him. And I— I couldn't deny the way Yash pulled at something in me—a feeling still too raw, too unformed to name.

A strange discomfort settled into my bones, creeping in quietly, curling into the spaces between my ribs like smoke. It wasn't jealousy. It couldn't be. It wasn't guilt. At least, not in the way I understood guilt.

But it was something. Something tangled and raw, something I wasn't ready to name.

I forced a nod, a small, careful smile—as if her words hadn't just shifted the ground beneath me. As if my pulse wasn't suddenly too loud in my ears.

"Just… be yourself," I said, my voice steady, even. A lie in its own way.

"He already likes talking to you. Maybe just give it time." Safe words. Neutral.

Something that didn't betray the fact that for the first time that night, I felt completely, utterly out of place.

Urmi grinned, nodding like I had just handed her the secret to something she had already been reaching for. Like this was just another harmless conversation between friends. Like I wasn't standing here, drowning in something I didn't quite understand.

I turned toward the mirror, fingers lifting to fix my hair—an excuse, a distraction. But in the reflection, I saw it. The way my hands trembled slightly. The way my expression faltered for a fraction of a second. The way my own eyes looked—not steady, not in control, but shaken.

I needed a moment. I needed to breathe. Because something had changed. And I wasn't ready for it. The air in the club felt heavier than before, thick with something unspoken, something shifting. The music throbbed through my skin, a steady, pulsating rhythm that I usually lost myself in. But tonight, it was just noise—just a blur in the background of something much more consuming.

We had barely returned to the table before I felt it— the quiet shift, the subtle but unmistakable change in the air between us.

Urmi leaned in toward Yash, her movements graceful, almost unconscious. There was an ease in her body language, the way she laughed, the way her eyes flickered toward him like she had done it a hundred times before. I had never noticed it before. Or maybe I had, and I just didn't want to see it.

But what unsettled me the most wasn't her. It was him. Because he wasn't looking at her. I felt the weight of it before I even lifted my eyes—the unmistakable intensity of his gaze settling on me.

It wasn't just a glance. It was intentional. Steady. Focused. Like a silent message meant for me and me alone. A second too long. A fraction too intense. The club, the people, the flashing neon lights—it all blurred into nothingness. Because in that moment, there was only him. And for the first time in a long time, I felt seen.

Not as someone's friend. Not as the woman who always had it together, always controlled, always self-contained. But as something more.

As a woman. As someone who could be wanted. The realization unraveled something inside me. I should have looked away. I should have ignored it. But I couldn't.

Because the longer I held his gaze, the more I recognized the hunger in it. Or maybe... maybe it was mine.

Urmi wasn't oblivious. She was many things—wild, carefree, impulsive—but she wasn't naive. She had always been intuitive in a way that unsettled me. And tonight was no different. She saw it. The charge in the air. The flicker of something undeniable passing between Yash and me.

In that instant, I watched her posture change. It was subtle, barely noticeable to anyone who wasn't paying attention. But I was.

The way she tilted her chin up just slightly, as if steeling herself. The way she pressed her lips together for half a second before stretching them into something that wasn't quite a smile.

And then, she spoke.

"Let's dance?" Light. Playful. But pointed. A challenge. A way to break the moment. A way to pull him back toward her. She knew what she was doing.

And suddenly, I was caught in the space that separated them—the conflict between what I should do and what I wanted to do, the pull between loyalty and desire. Because the truth was—I was sure—I didn't want to go with her. I wanted to be with Yash.

But I hesitated. And that hesitation was enough. I felt it before I even turned to him. Yash's eyes on me. Waiting. Watching.

And when I did finally look, his gaze didn't waver. He didn't say a word. He didn't have to. Because his expression said everything- Stay. Don't go. Don't let this moment break. The weight of that silent plea settled into my chest, sinking deep. It was irrational. It was reckless.

And yet, I couldn't ignore it.

Because the way he was looking at me— as if I was the only person around, as if he wasn't ready to let go of whatever was happening between us— was intoxicating in a way I hadn't prepared for.

And so, I didn't go. I rejected Urmi's offer to dance. And the moment I did, something in her expression flickered. She covered it well, masked it with an easy shrug, a casual "Suit yourself" before disappearing into the crowd.

But I had already seen it. A moment of hesitation. A moment of understanding. I knew—I had crossed a line I couldn't come back from. I didn't make an excuse. I didn't soften my refusal with a playful laugh or a half-hearted "maybe later." I just… didn't go. And that choice—mine and mine alone—hung in the air between us, heavy, irreversible.

Urmi's expression didn't change—not really. She was good at that, at masking emotions before they had the chance to fully form. But I saw the shift. Felt it. A flicker of something I couldn't quite name. And then, without hesitation, without a second glance, she turned away. She didn't argue, didn't push, just stepped onto the dance floor, merging with the rhythm like she'd always belonged to it, the pulse of the music swallowing her whole. As if it didn't matter. As if I didn't matter.

But I knew better. I felt the weight of my decision long after she disappeared into the crowd, long after the moment had passed. I had made a choice.

And for the first time that night, I wasn't sure if it was the right one.

Yash and I remained, our conversation uninterrupted. But something felt different. The way he looked at me. The world around us blurred—the chatter, the laughter, the swirl of neon lights flickering against the night sky. It all faded into nothingness, drowned beneath something far more consuming. Something unspoken.

His eyes—God, his eyes. They never left me. Not once. I wasn't imagining it. That steady, unreadable gaze. Like he was trying to figure me out, peeling away my layers without even asking for permission.

Like he already knew what I refused to admit to myself. That I wanted him to be mine. That I wanted to claim him in a way that wasn't logical, wasn't rational—but felt terrifyingly real.

I didn't want to think about Urmi. If that made me selfish, fine. I could live with that.

It's not like there was anything real between them. Not anything defined.

And yet—here I was, pulled toward him with a certainty that scared me a little. A feeling I hadn't asked for, hadn't planned. Still, it settled in me, low and sure.

I wasn't supposed to be here, standing this close, caught in a moment that felt too much like something.

She was the one who brought him into our world.

And yet, somehow, I felt like I belonged in this space with him more than she ever did.

The thought slid in before I could stop it—unwelcome, unkind. But true.

It lodged itself somewhere under my skin, quiet and heavy. And I let it stay.

And just when I thought I had a grip on myself, he spoke. "You okay?"

His voice was quiet, laced with something that felt dangerously close to concern. It slipped through the noise, cutting straight to me.

I blinked, willing myself to shake off the thoughts that had wrapped around my mind like vines. Too tight. Too consuming.

"Yeah…" The word felt unsteady, like it wasn't entirely mine. I cleared my throat, forcing a casual shrug. "We can just stand by the side and talk."

Like it was nothing. Like I wasn't faltering just a little. But he was still watching. And I wasn't sure if I wanted him to stop. He nodded once, reading between the lines without needing to be told. We stepped toward the edge of the rooftop, where the December air met us—crisp, cool, almost biting. I inhaled deeply, trying to steady myself, to clear my thoughts.

But then—his hand, light, barely there, resting against my back. Not pressing. Not demanding. Just… there. A quiet shield. A wordless reassurance. Something I didn't realize I had been craving. I should have moved away. But I didn't.

Because standing there, with him, wrapped in the glow of the city lights, in the safety of his presence, in the way he made the world feel smaller, quieter, safer—like it was second nature to him. — I didn't want to. It was happening. Slowly, quietly, like a tide pulling me under before I even had the chance to resist.

The way he listened—really listened. The way his laughter rumbled, rich and warm, spilling into the space between us. The way our conversation drifted, the kind that didn't feel like a beginning or an end—just something that had always existed.

I didn't even realize how much time had slipped away. Not until Urmi returned. And suddenly, the moment shattered, pulling me back to reality.

THE SHIFT IN THE AIR

The three of us lingered at the table, finishing off our drinks, absently picking at the last few fries and crumbs of whatever remained. No one was particularly hungry anymore, but habits were hard to break. The night had stretched long, wrapping around us with its easy conversations and unspoken tensions.

Eventually, we decided to leave. Descending the stairs to the ground floor, my eyes flickered across the familiar sea of faces—some regulars, some strangers. It was a ritual at ZEE, seeing people you'd seen before but never really knowing them beyond a nod or a fleeting smile.

And then, I saw him. Arun. Just a casual acquaintance. Someone I had spoken to before, in passing, over a drink or two on different nights. He wasn't a friend, not exactly. Just someone who existed in the same spaces as me often enough to warrant a familiar acknowledgment. He waved.

I stopped. It was nothing—just an easy greeting, an exchange of polite smiles. But somehow, the conversation stretched longer than expected, the small talk slipping into something easy and unplanned. A simple, harmless interaction. Or so I thought.

At first, I didn't notice it—the weight of his silence, the subtle shift in the air. The way the air around me thickened, electric with something unspoken. Yash hadn't said a word. Hadn't even moved.

But I felt it. The weight of him standing there. The sharp contrast between his usual ease and the way his presence felt heavier now.

Something had changed. He was watching. Not in a careless, passing way. Not in a way that invited questions or begged for explanations. But in a way that said he had seen enough. His body was still, too still—the kind of stillness that came before a storm.

He didn't interrupt. Didn't lean in. Didn't say a single thing. But the energy in the space between us had shifted, and suddenly, Arun's voice felt distant, muted, irrelevant. Because the real conversation was happening somewhere else. Wordless. Silent. Between me and Yash. Possessiveness. Not loud. Not forceful.

Just… there. A quiet kind of claim, wrapped in his silence. I knew this wasn't about Arun. It wasn't about trust. It was about the fact that, for those ten minutes, my attention hadn't been on him.

And that? That did not sit well with him.

I felt something twist in my stomach. Not guilt. Not unease. Something else. Something dangerously close to… satisfaction.

And just when I thought I had a handle on it—on him, on myself, on this moment—my eyes flickered past Yash.

And I saw her. Urmi. She was standing too close to him. Leaning in, just slightly. A whisper away. Close enough for her perfume to mix with the lingering smoke from his cigarette. Close enough that her fingers almost grazed his forearm as she gestured while speaking.

It was subtle. Almost nothing. But I knew Urmi. I knew her too well. Her movements weren't careless. They were practiced. Measured. It wasn't about flirting. It wasn't even about Yash.

It was about me. And she knew exactly what she was doing. The realization slammed into me, sharp and unrelenting. I wasn't the only one who had noticed the shift tonight. I wasn't the only one who felt the space between us closing in, suffocating in its intensity.

Urmi felt it too. And in that moment, the game was no longer the same. A beat of silence. A single, heavy second.

I turned back to Yash. He was still watching me. Still waiting. Still holding something in his eyes that I wasn't sure I was ready to see.

And suddenly, I wanted him to look at me the way he had been looking at me all night. Not at her. Me. It was reckless. It was selfish. And yet, standing there, caught between his silence, my growing need, and Urmi's carefully placed proximity—something inside me snapped.

I wanted him to be mine. Completely. Undeniably. Mine.

The night was winding down, but something in the air refused to settle. It lingered—unresolved, thick with things left unsaid. We stepped into the parking lot, the dim glow of the streetlights casting elongated shadows on the pavement. The night still carried the remnants of our laughter, the fading echo of conversations shared over beer and music.

And then, Urmi spoke. "I'm sitting in the front!"

It wasn't a casual statement. Not entirely. It was playful, light-hearted—but beneath the teasing, there was intent. A reclaiming. A restoration of something she felt had slipped through her fingers over the course of the night.

It was subtle, not desperate. Urmi wasn't the kind of woman to beg for space—she simply claimed it. With quiet grace, with disarming poise. She wasn't a girl who jumped and pouted; she was a woman who knew what she wanted and found a way to have it.

And yet—Yash moved first. With a single step, he reached the passenger door before she did, his actions unhurried, deliberate. Calmly certain, as always.

He pulled the door open—for me. "Sit," he said.

Not a suggestion. Not an offer. A quiet command. A statement of intent. I hesitated, just for a second. Not because I didn't want to. But because of what it meant.

Urmi hesitated too. A flicker. A brief moment of pause. And then, without a trace, it was gone. She masked it well—so well that anyone else would have missed it. The disappointment, the realization, the acceptance, wrapped neatly in a small, almost too light laugh.

"Fine, fine," she said, as if it didn't matter, as if she hadn't just been reminded of the shift between us. As if she hadn't noticed that tonight, something had changed. She moved toward the backseat without argument, her steps smooth, unhurried. She didn't push. Urmi wasn't someone who fought for a place that wasn't willingly given to her. But that didn't mean she hadn't felt it.

And I felt it too. I settled into the seat beside him, my body moulding into the familiar contours of the car.

Music filled the space almost instantly, spilling into the silence. The low hum of a song he liked, one he had played before. I barely registered the lyrics, too focused on the warmth that had taken residence inside the car, between us.

We talked—about the evening, about how good it had been, about how we needed more nights like this. The words came easy and natural. But beneath them, something else thrummed, an undercurrent. A quiet awareness.

And in the backseat, Urmi was watching. She didn't say much—not like she normally would. She wasn't someone who held back in conversations, who sat on the sidelines and let moments pass her by. She filled spaces with her presence, with her voice, with her energy.

But tonight? Tonight, she was careful. She watched instead, she was listening. I could feel it—her gaze flickering between Yash and me in the rearview mirror, picking up on the shifts we hadn't acknowledged aloud.

Reading between the spaces we thought were empty. I swallowed. Was I searching for meaning where there was none? Or was there something waiting to be seen?" Or had she sensed what I had spent the night trying not to name?

When we reached the metro stop where she had parked her two-wheeler, Yash slowed the car. I got down first, my movements instinctive, automatic. I paused before saying goodbye, I hugged her. "Good night," I murmured, squeezing her lightly, the gesture familiar. A habit.

She hugged me back, but her expression remained unreadable. No teasing remark. No playful jab about the night, about him. Just silence with a beat too long. And then, she turned—unlocking her bike, her back to me, the night swallowing whatever words she might have had.

Something in my chest tightened. Had something shifted between us? I didn't have time to answer that thought. Because before I could, I was already slipping back into the passenger seat—where Yash had told me to sit.

And as the car pulled away from the curb, the city lights flickering past us in a blur, one truth settled into my bones— Nothing about this night had been simple. And whatever had changed? The storm hadn't settled—it was only picking up speed.

A comfortable silence stretched between us as he drove, yet the air inside the car felt tense, fragile, like a delicate note hanging in the air, waiting to be played. Soft music played through the speakers, the volume just low enough to blend into the quiet hum of the engine. I hadn't noticed it at first, too lost in my thoughts. But now, as the night wrapped around us, I listened.

Anuv Jain.

The slow strumming of a guitar, vocals slipping easily into the spaces between us. I smiled to myself. I knew this song. The realization hit me like a quiet thrill—I hadn't expected our taste in music to align so seamlessly. It wasn't just the song—it was the feeling of it. The way it filled the car—calm, raw, familiar.

Was it intentional? Did he know I'd like it? I stole a glance at him, watching the way his fingers moved fluidly over the wheel, how his cologne lingered subtly in the space between us. The scent of him had already woven itself into my senses—cedarwood, musk, something deeper, something unmistakably him.

I turned my head toward the window, exhaling softly. This should have been easy. A drive home. A simple goodbye. But nothing about this felt simple anymore.

Too soon, we reached my place. The music faded as he cut the engine, the silence settling like something waiting to be acknowledged. He didn't say anything. Neither did I. And yet, the weight of the moment pressed against my skin, stretching between us in the small, dimly lit space of his car.

Finally, he smiled. That damn smile—the kind that was neither teasing nor polite, but something softer. Something unguarded. I exhaled, filling the pause between us with the only words I could manage. "Thank you."

I reached out instinctively, extending my hand for a handshake—because what else was I supposed to do? Keep sitting there, drowning in whatever this was? But before I could register what was happening, he leaned in. Not for my hand. For me.

In a way I didn't see coming—his arms were around me. A hug. Brief. Two, maybe three seconds. But God, what a hug. It wasn't just the warmth of him, or the way his body felt solid, certain, against mine. It was something else. Something that had already been decided, even if neither of us had spoken it aloud.

I didn't move. Didn't overthink. I just felt. The moment lingered, stretching beyond time, settling into the spaces where words felt unnecessary. I pulled away first. I had to. Because if I didn't, I might not have. He looked at me for a beat longer than necessary, something unreadable flickering in his eyes.

I told myself this was nothing. I told myself I was imagining the way his gaze felt different. But deep down, in the place where truths refused to be silenced, I knew—I wasn't. A part of me didn't want the night to end.

But then, the truth settled in. Urmi had feelings for him. And I wasn't meant to feel this way. So I smiled—casual, easy, as if my heart wasn't pounding in my ribs like a foolish, reckless teenager.

"Goodnight."

We parted ways, exchanging quiet goodbyes before he drove off. I stood there for a moment, watching his taillights fade into the distance, feeling something I couldn't quite name settle into my bones.

The second I stepped inside my house, a warmth spread through me—slow, consuming. And before I could stop it, I was smiling. Not a small, fleeting smile. No. A real one. A stupid, ridiculous, sixteen-year-old girl kind of grin.

I kicked off my heels, stretching into the quiet of my space, letting the night replay itself in my mind. I was still basking in the lingering warmth of the night, my mind floating somewhere between exhaustion and exhilaration.

And then— My phone buzzed.

Urmi: Reached home.

A second later, another message popped up.

Urmi: Did you enjoy?

I hesitated before replying. Not because I didn't know the answer, but because I wasn't sure how much I wanted to say. Hmm, yeah… he's different. He actually listens. It was the truth, yet it barely scratched the surface.

Before she could continue, I steered the conversation away. Feeling sleepy, will wash my face and sleep off. Talk to you tomorrow. I asked her, Whom should I pay?

Urmi: Yash paid.

I stared at the message for a second longer than necessary before typing back. Okay. Good night.

I placed my phone aside, moving through my night routine on autopilot—brushing my teeth, tying up my hair, washing my face with slow, deliberate strokes. And yet, my thoughts weren't quiet. I kept replaying the evening in my head—his voice, his presence, the way his eyes held mine like they had already learned a language I was just beginning to understand.

By the time I crawled into bed, my phone buzzed again. For some reason, I already knew who it was before I even looked.

Yash: Reached home. A simple message. Just two words. Yet, it was enough to make my chest tighten in a way I wasn't ready to admit.

I hesitated before typing back, my fingers moving instinctively. "How much do we owe you for the night?"

It was a simple question, a way to ground myself in normalcy. To keep things in their rightful place.

"No need," he replied.

I frowned. I insisted. Half-smiling to myself, I opened my payment app, determined to send my share. It was just a transaction, a courtesy, nothing more. But before I could complete it— Another message. Not from him. From Urmi. A screenshot.

My breath caught as I clicked on it, a flicker of unease curling in my stomach before I even read the words. A chat between Urmi and Yash. And there it was—clear, undeniable. He told her he liked me. Liked me? My grip on the phone tightened as my mind scrambled for a reaction. I should have expected this. Hadn't I felt it? Hadn't I sensed it in the way he looked at me, the way he listened, the way the air between us had changed?

But seeing it—seeing it confirmed in words—felt different. My heart stammered, my pulse fluttering in my throat as my fingers hovered over my keyboard. I could feel it—Urmi didn't like this. Not one bit. And why would she? She had seen it before I had. She had known before I let myself admit it.

I exhaled, the weight of it pressing against my ribs. Finally, I typed the only thing I could manage— "What is this that Urmi is saying?" His reply came almost instantly. "It is what it is. I really like you. It felt nice to be around you."

I stared at the screen, his words sinking in. There was no hesitation in them. No uncertainty, no half-heartedness. He had been sure. And Urmi had known it before I did.

Excitement flickered beneath my skin—brief, dangerous. But then, just as quickly, guilt seeped in. A strange mix of emotions spiralled through me—thrill, fear, anticipation, doubt. This wasn't casual. Or was it? This wasn't fleeting. Or was it?

And yet, I didn't know what it was supposed to be. I took a deep breath, my fingers hovering over the screen, uncertainty curling around my chest. I needed time. So I typed— "Good night, we'll talk in the morning. It's too late."

And with that, I put my phone away. I exhaled, sinking into my bed. But my mind refused to settle. My body was still humming from the night, from his gaze, from the way he had leaned in just a little closer than necessary.

From the hug that lingered longer than it should have, still warm against my skin, still there, like an unspoken promise. From the way I felt different—like something in me had already shifted, even if I wasn't ready to say it out loud.

And now, there was no denying it. Yash liked me. And I wasn't sure what that meant. I smiled to myself, a quiet, secret kind of happiness settling in. But beneath it, tangled in the warmth, was the weight of Urmi's disappointment. I wasn't supposed to feel this way. Not when she had wanted him first.

An hour passed. Maybe it was the beer. Maybe it was the exhaustion from the day. But eventually, my eyelids grew heavy, and finally, sleep took over.

RESTLESS ECHOES

The entire day passed in silence. No messages from Urmi. Nothing from Yash.

I kept checking my phone, half-expecting something—anything. A call, a message, even a forwarded meme that meant nothing but acknowledged everything. But there was nothing. Just an empty screen and a mind full of tangled thoughts.

Did Yash and Urmi talk? Did they sort things out? Did they... get together? The thought unsettled me, pressing against my ribs, making it harder to breathe. Should I message him? Should I call? Or should I just let it be?

But then, I reminded myself—he has a family. He must be busy with them. With his responsibilities, with his world that had nothing to do with me. And yet, the absence of his name lighting up my screen felt heavier than it should have.

And Urmi... how was she feeling? She must be hurt. Disappointed. I wouldn't want to be in her place. I shouldn't leave her like this. I should reach out. But would that make things better or worse?

Yet, in the middle of all these questions, all this uncertainty, there was one thing I couldn't ignore— The warmth of Yash's hug still lingered on me. The way his arms had wrapped around me, brief but certain. The way his eyes had searched for mine. The way I felt so at ease with him, as if I had known him far longer than I actually had.

And that thought alone... It made me smile. I shouldn't be smiling. The evening stretched long before I finally found the courage to call Urmi. I told her Yash didn't mean anything by it—that there was nothing to it. A lie. A lie I was telling her. A lie I was telling myself.

But for what? To escape what? The truth? The truth that I longed for him, that I wanted him to call me, to ask me how I felt. That I wanted him to say, forget everything else. Let's just see where this goes.

But instead, I asked Urmi what she wanted. She laughed—her usual, carefree laugh—but it felt different this time. Stretched. Hollow.

"It's your life," she said. "Do whatever makes you happy. I'm out of this."

Then, softer, almost to herself— "History repeats, huh?"

And in that moment, it hit me. Back in college, she had been in the same situation. She had liked a guy, but that guy had liked her friend instead. Guilt settled deep in my chest. This wasn't fair to her.

This wasn't how things were supposed to happen. I made up my mind. I would call Yash and tell him I had no feelings for him. I picked up my phone and messaged him: Are you free?

His reply came almost instantly. "What happened?", He asked

"I want to talk to you about last night." I said

"Give me ten minutes. Call me then," He replied

I paced, my thoughts spinning, then finally went up to my terrace and dialed his number.

We spoke for almost thirty minutes. At first, the words came easily. I don't like you. Urmi likes you. I can't betray her. He listened. Patient. Quiet. And then, before I could stop myself, the question slipped out.

"That night… the night you and Urmi stayed at your place, drinking. Did something happen?" There was a pause. "Was there ever anything between you and Urmi?"

Silence stretched between us, thick and unspoken. He exhaled. Slow. Measured. Like he had been waiting for this. Then, his voice—steady, calm. "Nothing happened."

"She seemed different after that. Almost like she expected something more." I said, the words lingering longer than I intended.

"It wasn't like that. We were just two neighbors having a drink. That's it. Like neighbors do. Like friends do. Like colleagues who catch up after a long day, share a drink, exchange a few laughs, and part ways without a second thought.

"If there was anything between us—if something had actually happened—I wouldn't have told her last night that I liked you. That alone should tell you everything. It's really that simple."

He said it so plainly, like it was the most obvious thing in the world. And maybe, for him, it was.

I wanted to believe him. I did believe him. But none of this was just casual anymore. Not for Urmi. Not for me. I searched for something in his tone—hesitation, regret, a flicker of uncertainty. But there was nothing.

Yash wasn't the kind of man who twisted words. He wasn't the kind who sugarcoated things or left room for doubt. He said what he meant. And he meant what he said.

"It was always that simple," he continued. "I never hid anything, it is what it is."

The certainty in his voice should have settled something in me. It should have made things easier. But it didn't. Because now, the only thing left to question was myself.

"We should stop talking," I told him, pushing the words out before I lost my nerve. "This… whatever this is… I can't do this. Urmi is my friend. She's been in this place before. I won't be the reason she feels like that again."

He didn't argue. He didn't try to convince me otherwise. He just listened. And then, after a long pause— He exhaled, as if reading my thoughts. "Look, I can't force you to like me. But yes, I like you. And I'm not going to pretend I don't."

His words hung between us, settling into the spaces I had tried so hard to ignore. A confession so simple, so stark, that my breath caught in my throat. And then, softer—like he was offering me a choice, not a demand— "But it's your call."

It was always my call. Because unlike me, he was clear. He knew what he wanted. I was the one who didn't. Him, standing his ground. Me, trying to pretend I wasn't tempted to stay. Neither of us willing to budge. I liked him this way. No "ifs" or "buts." No games. No confusion. Just clarity. Something I had never been good at giving myself.

"Good night, Yash," I murmured, feeling something slip through my fingers.

"Good night," he replied. In a quiet decision, we decided— No more calls. No more messages. Silence.

But as I ended the call, staring at the dark sky above me, a sharp ache settled in my chest. Because even though I had walked away first… it didn't feel like I had won anything. It felt like I had just lost something I wasn't ready to lose. I shook the thoughts away.

No point in overthinking. No point in holding on to something that was already slipping away. With a deep breath, I turned and headed back to my apartment, letting the night swallow whatever was left of the conversation.

The next morning, I woke up feeling strange—somewhere between relief and regret. I had done the right thing. Hadn't I? But the weight in my chest didn't feel like victory. It felt like something unfinished. Something unresolved.

My mind kept replaying the conversation with Yash, the way his voice had lingered in my thoughts long after we hung up. The way he had said, "I can't force you to like me, but I do like you."

I tried to shake it off, tried to will myself to forget, but it clung to me like a shadow.

At work, over coffee, I spilled everything to Tina. She listened, the way she always did, her eyes sharp with understanding, her presence steady like an anchor against the chaos in my head.

"Yash says there's nothing between them," I sighed, stirring my drink absentmindedly. "Should I believe him?"

Tina didn't even hesitate. "If he's saying it, then yes, you should."

Her certainty made me pause. I bit my lip, my mind still tangled in knots. "But what about Urmi? What if I came in between them? What if I—"

"Stop right there," Tina cut me off, her eyes locking onto mine with that unwavering clarity she always had.

"You're overthinking this. Feelings don't follow rules. Anybody can have feelings for anyone. Anyone can love anyone. But a relationship? That takes two people who choose each other. And Yash? He's choosing you, not her."

Her words settled something deep inside me. A truth I had been avoiding. Yash was choosing me. So why did I feel guilty? I exhaled, feeling lighter, as if some of the weight had lifted off my chest. Talking to her always had that effect.

Days slipped by. Soon, it was the New Year. I hadn't spoken to Yash since that night. Hadn't messaged him. Hadn't reached out. But he was there, in the spaces between my thoughts, in the moments where I least expected him.

On a whim, I sent him a message—"Happy New Year!"

My heart drummed a little faster than it should have as I stared at the screen.

His reply came almost instantly. "Happy New Year to you too."

A small conversation unfolded—light on words, heavy with everything left between the lines. "How was your New Year's Eve?" I asked.

"Nothing much, just with family. You?"

"Spent it with family and cousins. A lot of drinking, a lot of celebrating."

A pause. A beat too long.

"Sounds fun."

Without warning, the chat ended. Short. Simple. But it left a whisper of anticipation in its wake, lingering in the quiet spaces of my mind. He still wanted to talk to me. That meant something. Didn't it? A couple of days later, my phone buzzed. A message.

Yash- "Hey."

My heart did an embarrassing little jump. I stared at the screen for a second longer than necessary before typing back—"Hi." "Long time? What's up?" I added, trying to keep it casual.

Yash- "Can we meet?" The question hung there, simple yet loaded with meaning.

I didn't hesitate. "Sure."

In the blink of an eye, the silence between us broke. The decision came before the thought. Before the logic. Before the guilt. It was instinctive, immediate—the kind of decision that wasn't really a decision at all. It just… happened.

Excitement bubbled up inside me, unchecked and unfiltered, spreading through my veins like wildfire. The mere idea of seeing him again sent a thrill through me, an electric pulse I had no control over. I barely even registered the fact that Urmi hadn't crossed my mind until much later. But even when I did, I didn't stop myself.

Over the past week, she'd been busy. Distant, even. Our conversations had thinned into small, passing exchanges, the kind that felt obligatory rather than intentional. And, truthfully? I wasn't trying to change that.

I didn't tell her I was meeting Yash. Not because I forgot. But because some part of me didn't want to. Some part of me knew that saying it out loud would make it real. Would force me to acknowledge something I wasn't ready to admit—that I wanted this. That I wanted him.

The next evening, as the sun dipped lower into the horizon, my phone buzzed.

Yash: "I'll pick you up."

I hesitated for a second before replying. "Do you remember where I stay?"

Yash: "Just share the location anyway."

Something about that made me pause. It took me back—to the evening I first met him. With Urmi. The memory surfaced too easily, as if it had been waiting for a moment like this. As if it had never really left me.

I had always dressed up when I went out—carefully choosing outfits, making sure every detail was right. But with him, that first time... I hadn't felt the need to. For the first time, I felt comfortable just being. Just me.

I stood in front of my wardrobe again, staring at the rows of clothes, but the decision was easy. A simple t-shirt and jeans. Nothing fancy. Nothing extra. Just me. A few minutes later, my phone rang.

"Reaching in five."

"I'll be down," I replied, slipping on my sneakers.

I stepped outside just as his car pulled up. And then I saw him. Something in my chest tightened. His eyes. Just like before—dark, unreadable, yet pulling me in before I could even think. His scent- clean, crisp, and unmistakably him.

He was wearing a white shirt, slightly crumpled from what must have been a long, exhausting day at work, paired with blue jeans. Simple, undone in the best way. But somehow, he still looked devastatingly good. The kind of good that made my stomach flutter in a way I refused to acknowledge.

His dark, black curls fell slightly over his forehead, unruly yet perfect. Without me even realizing—He had me. Again. How did he do this? How did he make me feel completely insane without even trying? I took a slow breath, steadying myself. And then, I got into the car. As soon as I settled into the seat, he turned to me with a soft smile.

"Hey," he said, his voice warm—low, steady, like it knew how to hold your attention without asking for it.

And before I could think—before I could prepare for what was coming— He pulled me into a hug. It lasted only two or three seconds—brief, fleeting. But in that moment? It felt like forever.

I never liked hugs from strangers, they made me uncomfortable—always had. My friends knew that. Some of them even hugged me just to irritate me.

I've been hugged before. Of course, I have. I have a family. People who love me.

There have been embraces exchanged in celebration, in greeting, in comfort. But somewhere along the way, in the rush of life and all its responsibilities, you forget the basic language of love. You forget what it means to stop. To hold. To be held.

A hug becomes a habit. A quick gesture. Something you give in passing, like small change at a crowded counter. Or it disappears altogether. We take people for granted. Or we run out of time. Or both.

And then there was him. I had felt the warmth of a hug before. But not like this.

Not the kind that wrapped around you, not just in touch—but in feeling. In intention.

Like his arms weren't just there to hold my body, but every part of me I'd kept tucked away. He hugged me like he meant it. Like he knew exactly how much I needed it—even when I didn't.

His arms around me felt less like an action and more like a place. A place I'd somehow forgotten I was allowed to return to. With him, it wasn't just warmth. It wasn't obligation or habit. It was quiet, wordless understanding. A steady heartbeat against mine. A breath let out after holding it for too long.

And in that space—pressed to his chest, his hand tracing slow circles on my back—I realized something I didn't want to admit until then. That I'd been starving for something this simple. That I had taught myself not to need it. And yet, here I was. Unlearning all of that in the silence of his arms.

His hug didn't just feel safe. It felt like home. Like life. Like something I could believe in. Even if it wasn't perfect. Even if it wasn't permanent. For those moments, it was everything.

And no matter how much I fought it—no matter how much I told myself I didn't believe in things like this, in moments like this, in something unspoken like this— Somewhere deep inside, I knew. I wanted to.

Soft music played in the background, blending seamlessly with the quiet hum of the car. It wasn't loud, just enough to fill the silence between us, making everything feel a little more intimate. The kind of intimacy that sneaks up on you—not forced, not intentional, just there.

Yash's fingers tapped lightly against the steering wheel, his movements easy, familiar. He stole a glance at me, a hint of amusement dancing in his eyes. "Where to?" he asked.

Then, before I could answer, he smirked. "Same place—ZEE?"

His tone was teasing, playful, like he already knew the answer, like he was teasing me the way only he could—

light, knowing, close. I turned to him, narrowing my eyes. "Why? You didn't like it?"

I wasn't sure why I asked. Maybe I wanted to know if he had enjoyed our last time there as much as I did. Maybe I just wanted to hear him say it. He shrugged. "The place is okay. Didn't like the food, though. Can we go somewhere else?"

"Sure," I said, pulling out my phone to look for options.

As I scrolled through places, I noticed the music in the background getting louder. At first, I thought it was my imagination. But then—no, it was definitely increasing. I glanced at him with a knowing smile, ready to call him out for messing with the volume. And that's when I saw him.

There he was—completely lost in the music, his fingers drumming lightly against the steering wheel, his lips moving, unthinking, like the words had always been his. And then, it hit me. He was singing. Not just mouthing the words. Singing.

His voice—rich, smooth, completely at ease—filled the car. He wasn't trying. He wasn't performing. He was just… singing. And he was good. Like, unfairly good. I stared, realization crashing into me like a wave. God, he's not just good-looking. He sings too? It almost felt unfair—how someone could be this undeniably good-looking and also sound this good. I didn't even realize I was still staring until he caught me.

He smirked, one eyebrow arching in that infuriatingly self-assured way of his. "What?"

I quickly looked back at my phone, biting back a smile. "Nothing." But my heart? It was beating a little faster than before. I cleared my throat, forcing myself to focus. "How about Roots?" I suggested.

He turned to me, one hand still on the steering wheel. "Have you been there before?"

"No," I admitted.

He nodded. "Fine, let's go. It's close by, and we don't have to deal with too much traffic."

It was a practical decision. Simple. No debate, no unnecessary back-and-forth. But something about the ease of it—the way he just agreed, the way he trusted my choice without hesitation—made me smile.

BARE AND BREAKING

We reached the place and asked for a table for two. The host led us outside to a cozy corner table, tucked away amidst lush greenery. The kind of spot that made you want to sit a little longer, breathe a little slower.

The soft hum of conversations, the dim glow of string lights, the crisp January air—it all felt… perfect. The kind of setting that made everything feel lighter, unhurried.

I barely had time to soak it all in before Yash leaned back in his chair with a dramatic sigh. "I'm starving," he groaned. "I need food."

I laughed, shaking my head. "I feel like this is the first time you've actually admitted it. Usually, you pretend to be all calm and put-together." He grinned, completely unapologetic. "Yeah, well. Good food is important. And I trust you'll order something decent."

I rolled my eyes, flipping open the menu. "No pressure at all, huh?"

He smirked but said nothing, letting me take the lead. And in that moment—between his quiet amusement, the gentle music in the background, and the warmth of the setting—I realized something.

I liked this. Not just him. Not just the way he made my heart race when he looked at me a certain way. But this. The ease. The familiarity. The feeling of knowing someone without really knowing them. The way the night stretched ahead, unhurried, like there was nowhere else we needed to be but here.

I exhaled deeply, trying to steady myself as I flipped through the menu. Someone stop me, I thought—I could feel myself slipping away, and I had no way of holding on. A nervous laugh escaped me, and we both began scanning the menu. The familiar routine kicked in as we made our selections, the chatter about the food making everything feel just a little more normal. I didn't even realize how much I needed that normalcy until it was right there in front of me."

While we waited, I found myself watching him—taking in the way he sat back, completely at ease, fingers idly tapping against the table. There was a stillness to him—anchored, unreadable. Like nothing touched him, or maybe everything did and he just didn't show it.

Yash was the kind of guy who was completely unbothered by pretense. He spoke his mind without hesitation, always raw and honest. There were no filters with him—if he liked something, he didn't hold back. If he didn't, it was just as clear. He never wasted time trying to impress anyone or pretending to be someone he wasn't. He was refreshingly real, always exactly who he said he was. And yet, despite his bluntness, there was something so easy about being around him—like he had this rare ability to make you feel comfortable just by existing.

Then, something struck me. Last time, he had gone through almost half a dozen cigarettes. But today? Not a single one. I tilted my head and asked, "No cigarettes today?"

He glanced at me, then stretched his arms lazily. "Nahhh…" he said with an easy shrug, his voice slow, unbothered. There was something about the way he said it, the way he looked just then—so unguarded, so stripped of anything performative—just him, as he was.

And in that instant, I realized something. I was falling for him. Not in a way that made my heart race uncontrollably. Not in a way that felt overwhelming or all-consuming. No. It was quiet. Unspoken. A slow pull, like a tide inching forward before you even notice you're knee-deep in the ocean. And yet, it was happening.

We talked about everything—work, toxic colleagues, life, ambitions, music. Time slipped through our fingers, unnoticed, as words passed freely between us, unfiltered and easy. Soft music played in the background, blending into the hum of the night. The dim lights cast a warm glow around us, flickering slightly in the evening breeze. The January air carried the faint scent of grilled food and something else—something unspoken that lingered between us.

Somewhere between our laughter and our quiet pauses, we ended up reordering the same soya chaap he had absolutely loved. It felt easy. Familiar. Like we had done this a hundred times before. And maybe, just maybe— I wanted to do it a hundred times more.

And then—at some point—I hadn't even noticed when—he reached for my hand. His fingers found mine, settling there with the gentleness of something familiar. And I didn't pull away. I didn't want to. His touch was gentle but sure, like a quiet promise neither of us spoke aloud. A soft current passed through me, subtle yet undeniable. I let my thumb graze his just slightly—a silent way of saying, I'm okay with this.

I wanted to pretend I wasn't affected, that this wasn't doing something to me. But the music, the lights, the warmth of him so close—it all wove into something deeper, something that made me want more of this. More of him.

But then, discomfort began creeping into my back. I shifted slightly, trying to ease the dull ache that had settled there. He noticed immediately.

"Long day at work?" he asked, his voice quieter now, laced with concern.

I sighed. "Yeah… had to anchor an event. Was standing and hosting for hours."

He studied me for a second, as if debating something. And then, without hesitation, he got up from his seat and sat next to me. Close. Close enough that the warmth of him chased away the evening chill. Close enough that

I knew—without a doubt—I was falling deeper into something I wasn't sure I could walk away from.

He stretched his hand across my back, his fingers pressing gently, searching. His eyes stayed on me, unreadable yet knowing. "Here?" he asked, his voice low, almost a whisper.

A shiver ran down my spine. I swallowed and nodded. He understood.

Without another word, he continued, his touch firm yet careful, easing the tension in my muscles, replacing it with something else entirely. Something that made my breath catch.

"Feeling better?" he asked after a moment.

I wanted to tell him no. To tell him not to stop. But that would make me sound desperate. So instead, I forced a small smile. "Yeah… better. You don't have to do this." But my body betrayed me—my breath uneven, my pulse just a little too fast under his touch.

I didn't want him to notice, so I grabbed my drink— anything to distract myself. And in my haste, I knocked the entire glass over. The cold liquid splashed onto the table, soaking my jeans.

"Oh no!" I gasped, my eyes widening. What did I just do?

But before the embarrassment could fully settle in, he chuckled. Not just a small laugh—a full, amused, utterly unbothered laugh. He shook his head, eyes dancing with mischief. Instead of making me feel awkward, he made me feel… at ease. Like it was no big deal.

We called for the hostess, who quickly directed us to another table. "It's the only one available," she said, leading us to a spot tucked away in a darker, cozier corner.

Yash glanced at me, a question in his eyes. "Is this okay?"

I exhaled, still flustered from everything. "No choice," I muttered, making him grin.

Somewhere between then and now, the tension shifted into something else. Something warmer. Something that made me want to stay in this moment a little longer. This time, he didn't sit across from me. He sat next to me. Close enough that our arms brushed slightly, close enough that his presence wrapped around me like an unspoken promise.

We continued talking—about everything and nothing, our conversation flowing like it had a life of its own. But I wasn't just listening anymore. I was watching him. The way his lips moved when he spoke. The way his eyes flickered with amusement, curiosity, something deeper.

Maybe he noticed. Maybe he saw the way my gaze lingered a little too long, the way my breath hitched ever so slightly whenever he leaned in. I wasn't saying it out loud. But I was giving him hints—subtle, undeniable.

I had a strong, sudden urge to kiss him. It came out of nowhere—wild, uninvited, and impossible to ignore. To pull me into that same hug he'd given me earlier—those fleeting two or three seconds that had lived in my skin long after they ended.

But this time, I wanted longer. This time, I wanted more.

Something inside me was burning. A quiet, insistent ache that only grew stronger the longer I sat next to him.

I wanted him. Not just physically—though that pull was undeniable—but in a way that felt raw and unexpected. Like some part of me had been waiting for this exact moment to come undone.

And the way his gaze lingered, the way the air seemed to thicken between us—I knew he could feel it too.

The air between us was thick with something unspoken, something just waiting to shatter the space still left between us. We didn't even realize the world around us had faded. It was just us—lost in conversation, in stolen glances, in the electricity that crackled in the spaces between.

The hostess approached with an apologetic smile. "We're closing now."

I blinked, momentarily disoriented. Closing? A quick glance at my phone told me the truth—I had spent nearly five hours with him. And yet, it didn't feel like enough.

Reluctantly, we settled the bill and stepped outside, the night air crisp against my skin.

"Where's your car?" I asked.

"Valet," he replied.

The valet directed us a little ahead, saying it was just a short walk. So we walked. Side by side.

With every step, I could feel his arm brushing against my bare skin, sending shivers down my spine. Each accidental touch ignited something reckless, something that made me want him to just stop walking— To turn to me. To pull me close. To close the unbearable distance between us. But he didn't. We reached the car. He unlocked it, and we slipped inside.

But he didn't start the engine. He just sat there. And so did I. And in that moment, the silence wasn't just silence. It was everything. The air between us thickened, loaded with everything we had left unsaid.

I turned to him, my voice teasing but softer now. "What?" I asked. "Don't want to go?"

He exhaled, his gaze never leaving mine. "No. I just... I wish time could stop." His voice was quiet, but the weight of those words settled deep inside me. And for a moment, I let them.

And then—slowly, deliberately—he leaned in. His hand traced its way to my waist, fingers pressing just enough to make me aware of his touch—gentle yet certain, as if committing every curve, every inch of me to memory. It wasn't rushed. It wasn't hesitant. It was the kind of touch that made time stretch, that made my skin hum with anticipation.

His breath—warm, intoxicating—ghosted over my lips, the faintest tease of a sensation that wasn't quite there, yet consumed me entirely. My pulse quickened, each second stretching impossibly long. His eyes, dark and unreadable, searched mine—not demanding, not pleading, just waiting.

Waiting for permission. Waiting for surrender. Waiting for me to meet him halfway. And I didn't make him wait. I leaned in too, drawn to him like gravity, my fingers sliding instinctively to the back of his neck. The softness of his curls tangled between my fingers, warm and alive, a contrast to the heat simmering between us. My touch tightened slightly, not pulling him closer—just feeling him, grounding myself in the moment before it slipped away.

His scent—God, his scent—wrapped around me, familiar now, yet still intoxicating. A mix of something fresh, something dark, something uniquely him. It clung to the air between us, to my skin, to the space we had unknowingly created.

And then, in the next breath, we kissed. Soft at first. Slow. A delicate testing of waters. A question, an unspoken *are we really doing this?* that neither of us needed to answer. His lips—warm, firm—moved against mine, hesitant for only a fleeting second before deepening, before finding the rhythm that had always been there, waiting to be claimed. The faintest brush of his tongue sent a shiver through me, a quiet sigh slipping past my lips, betraying me before I even realized I was breathing him in.

Everything else—time, place, consequence—blurred into irrelevance. All that remained was this. For a few perfect seconds, nothing else existed.

Then, reality nudged its way back in. We pulled away—just barely, just enough to breathe. A quiet smile played on his lips. Mine mirrored his. But our eyes? Our eyes said we wanted more.

I exhaled, still catching my breath. "What an absolutely wonderful time I had."

He grinned, mischief flickering in his eyes. "So soon?"

I barely had time to react—before I could think, before I could even respond—he leaned in again and then I heard the soft click as he pushed the car seat back—creating space. For me. For him. For this.

He made sure I was comfortable. He adjusted, without words, to make room for both of us—to move closer, to close the gap that had felt electric just seconds before. And then he kissed me. This time, the kiss was deeper. Longer. A kiss unlike anything I had ever experienced before—jolting, electrifying, awakening something inside me that I didn't even know existed. Not that I hadn't kissed before. But his kiss? It felt different. Like I belonged to him. And he, to me.

And then, without a word, he trailed downward.

His mouth brushed along my jaw, unhurried, reverent. And when his lips reached my neck—God—I forgot how to breathe.

The first kiss there was soft. Barely a whisper against my skin. But it sent a jolt through me, a shiver that danced down my spine. Then another—firmer this time. A lingering press, his breath warm and heavy against my throat.

My head tilted on instinct, surrendering, giving him space I didn't even realize I was offering. It was a reflex, a need. Like my body already knew exactly where it wanted him.

He kissed the spot just below my ear, and I felt my hands tighten around him, anchoring myself to the only solid thing in that moment—him. His lips grazed lower, his stubble brushing against the sensitive skin of my collarbone, setting off sparks I couldn't contain.

His mouth moved with purpose, like he was claiming territory. Not rough, not hurried—but hungry. And every kiss left a mark I'd carry long after this night ended—not just on my skin, but somewhere deeper.

The heat between us wasn't just rising anymore. It was surging.

And I wanted more. More of his mouth. More of that fire. More of him.

My hands found his shoulders, gripping him as his lips moved against mine with a slow, deliberate hunger. His fingers traced along my waist, slipping beneath my soft T-shirt, his touch igniting trails of heat on my skin.

And strangely, I didn't stop him. I didn't want to stop him. Because for once, someone was holding me. Not because they expected something from me. Not because it was an obligation. But simply because they wanted to.

Fingertips glided along my back, tracing invisible patterns against my skin, igniting shivers that curled down my spine. A featherlight graze, a teasing pause— his hands read me like a story, one he was in no hurry to finish.

Then, higher. The moment his fingers brushed against my breasts, a sharp inhale caught in my throat, my body betraying me before I could even process what I was feeling. A slow, deliberate stroke—a quiet exploration— sent waves of sensation rolling through me, pooling in places I hadn't realized were waiting.

It wasn't just touch. It was presence. A moment suspended outside of time, outside of logic. A moment where nothing existed beyond the warmth of his hands, the weight of his body against mine, the unspoken intensity that neither of us dared to name.

The world had faded. As though we were lost somewhere, untethered from reality.

I found myself craving more—the warmth of him, the way he touched me, the way every glance, every kiss felt like an unraveling of something neither of us had fully understood yet. My body moved on instinct, my desires overriding reason, hesitation no longer a part of the equation.

Without a second thought, I slipped my hands beneath his crumpled white shirt, my fingers seeking the heat of his skin. The moment I touched him, I felt it—his body, taut beneath my fingertips, firm, sculpted, radiating a quiet strength. His muscles tensed at the sensation, as if my touch had ignited something within him that even he hadn't expected.

And then—his breath hitched.

It was barely audible, just the smallest shift in his breathing, but I felt it more than I heard it. That single, sharp intake of air, that moment of pause before he exhaled again—it sent a rush of satisfaction through me. I was affecting him the way he was affecting me.

His fingers tangled in my hair, threading through the strands with a reverence that made my stomach tighten. He tilted my head back just slightly, deepening the kiss— his lips moving against mine with a hunger that was growing, intensifying, taking. And I let him.

My hands wandered, memorizing the shape of him, tracing the hard lines of his back, the smooth expanse of his chest. Every inch of him felt like something crafted with intention, strong yet yielding beneath my touch.

God, what a body. It was unfair, almost. The way he felt, the way he moved, the way he fit against me like this was something inevitable. I could feel his heartbeat now, hammering against mine, rapid, breathless. Our breaths tangled, merging into one, the space between us vanishing entirely.

The world outside? It didn't exist. Nothing else mattered. Just him. Just us. Just this moment—stretched between want and need, between now and forever.

And then— A faint honk shattered the silence, snapping us back to reality.

We stopped. I exhaled, tucking my hair behind my ear, trying to steady myself. He ran a hand through his curls, a careless gesture that made him even more impossible to ignore.

I broke the silence first. "Let's go?"

He looked at me, his gaze lingering.

"I don't want the night to end."

My heart clenched at the honesty in his voice.

"I don't either," I admitted, "but we have to."

A beat of silence. Then, as if the thought had been sitting on my tongue all along, I asked, "Can we meet again?"

A small smile played at his lips. "Yes. Of course."

With that, he started the car. The music filled the space again, the volume creeping up like it had a mind of its own. And as we drove into the night, my fingers tingled where his had been, my lips still warm from his kiss.

I smiled to myself. I'd noticed this about him. The way he blasted music without apology, sang like no one was listening, like the world outside the car didn't exist. And God, he sang so well. How could someone be so effortlessly disarming? So beautifully unaware of how easy he was to fall into?

The drive back felt too short. Soon, we reached my apartment. He pulled the car into a dark spot near my gate, his movements slower now, as if stalling.

For a second, he glanced outside, checking if anyone was watching. And then, without a word, he leaned in again. A soft, quick kiss on my warm lips. A kiss that said this isn't over.

"I'll call you," he murmured.

I nodded. "Drop me a message once you reach home."

With one last lingering look, I stepped out, my heartbeat still racing.

I climbed into bed, but sleep was the last thing on my mind. My phone stayed close, my fingers mindlessly refreshing our chat.

Would he text? Was he thinking about me too?

Twenty minutes later, my phone buzzed.

Yash: Just reached home.

Relief washed over me. I smiled, typing back.

Me: Sleep tight. Good night.

A moment passed. Then another buzz.

Yash: Tonight felt special.

My heart flipped. I stared at the screen, rereading his words, feeling the warmth of them sink into me. It was special. More than he even knew.

A PAUSE IN THE NOISE

That night, sleep felt impossible. Somewhere in between losing myself in Yash's thoughts, I drifted into sleep, his touch, his voice, and his lingering scent still wrapped around me like a dream I never wanted to wake up from.

But the next morning, reality felt different—like I was walking through the day with a secret pressed against my skin. At work, I found myself lost in thought, contemplating whether to tell Tina or not.

Half a day had passed, and the words sat heavy on my tongue, waiting—begging—to be spoken. But I was scared. Scared of Tina's reaction. Scared of what she might think of me. Scared of what I might think of myself.

I had never been the woman who lost herself over a man. Never been the woman who let herself get swept up in feelings, in emotions, in things that had no place in my life.

I had responsibilities. A job. A family. A life I had carefully built around stability, control, practicality. And yet, here I was—refreshing his messages, replaying his touch, feeling recklessly happy in a way I hadn't allowed myself to feel in years.

What if Tina didn't understand? What if she reminded me of what I already knew?

That feeling wasn't magic. It was effort, expectation, responsibility.

I had seen what connections became over time. I had lived it.

I wasn't the kind of woman who believed in grand emotions.

Not anymore.

I toyed with my coffee cup, my fingers hovering over our chat, re-reading the messages from last night. My heart still raced at his words. A part of me wanted to tell her everything—to spill the butterflies in my stomach, the way his touch had set my skin on fire, the way I had lost track of time with him. But another part held back.

Tina knew me too well. She had already sensed something was off, the way my mind kept drifting, the way I smiled to myself for no reason.

This morning, when I first saw her, she had asked casually, "How was last night?" I had shrugged, keeping it short. "It was good."

She had narrowed her eyes at me, unconvinced. But she let it go. For now.

For hours, I dodged her. Buried myself in work. Pretended to be too busy to talk. But I could feel her watching me, waiting for me to crack. And then, during our coffee break, she finally snapped.

"Okay, spill—what is it?" she demanded, setting her cup down with a sharp thud.

"Did he disappoint you? Did he say something? Or wait… did Urmi come?"

Her questions came fast, impatient, her eyes locked onto mine. I froze. My heart pounded. There was no escaping now. Before she could ask any further or assume the worst, I spilled it. Well, not all of it. I kept it simple.

"We kissed," I said, stirring my coffee. "Nothing else."

Tina raised an eyebrow, her expression calm yet knowing. She wasn't the type to giggle like a schoolgirl or pry unnecessarily, but I could tell she was reading between the lines.

"Just a kiss?" she asked, her voice measured.

I nodded, trying to seem casual, but the way I fidgeted with my sleeve betrayed me. Even now, sitting across from her, I could still feel Yash—his breath warm against my neck, his fingers tracing my waist, his hands tangled in my hair. He wasn't here, but somehow, every inch of him still lingered on me.

Tina exhaled, giving me a small, amused smile. "You don't have to say it, you know," she said, sipping her coffee. "It's written all over your face."

I let out a quiet laugh, shaking my head. "God, is it that obvious?" She smirked. "You have a glow, babe. And I'm not talking about good skincare."

I rolled my eyes, but I couldn't help but smile. There was something comforting about Tina—how she never judged, never pressed too hard, just let me exist in my emotions without making me feel silly about them.

Then, in a softer tone, she added, "I'm really glad you're happy."

I looked at her then, truly looked at her, and realized how much I had needed to hear that. Because for the first time in a long time— I truly was.

Just then, my phone buzzed.

Yash: At work?

I felt a small smile tug at my lips as I typed back.

Me: Yes.

A moment later, another message popped up.

Yash: How's it going?

I stared at the screen for a second, my fingers hovering over the keyboard. It was a simple question, but the way it made my heart skip felt anything but simple.

Me: It's okay. A bit distracted, though.

I hesitated before hitting send, wondering if he'd pick up on the hint. A typing bubble appeared almost instantly. I barely had a second to process before his reply popped up.

Yash: Yeah, I know. I'm too irresistible.

I rolled my eyes, but I couldn't stop the grin spreading across my face. I could practically see him smirking through the screen, that cocky edge wrapped in a kind of laid-back confidence that came through with every word. I loved his playfulness. It was a breath of fresh air—so easy, so natural.

Me: Oh, absolutely. It's a real problem.

I hit send, biting my lip, waiting for his comeback.

Yash: Ok, I'll call after work?

Me: I'll wait.

The moment I hit send, I felt a warmth spread through me. The anticipation, the way my heart raced—it was all so new, yet so intoxicating.

Tina, who had been watching me the entire time, smiled knowingly. She didn't say a word. Just stood up, tapped my shoulder, and with a smirk, said, "Alright, lovebird. Back to work."

I let out a small laugh, shaking my head as she walked away. But as I turned back to my screen, my mind was anywhere but work. All I could think about was the night before.

His touch, his voice, the way he looked at me like I was the only person in the world. And now, all I could do was wait for the day to end, to get back home, and to hear his voice again.

The day crawled by at work, every hour stretching longer than usual. By the time evening came, I had busied myself with chores at home, trying not to keep glancing at my phone. But then, it rang. His name lit up my screen.

I answered instantly, my heart skipping a beat. We talked for 30 minutes—just easy, flowing conversation, laughter woven in between. Nothing too deep, nothing too complicated.

Yet, every word felt like a thread pulling me closer to him. I didn't know where this would lead, didn't overthink what it meant. All I knew was that, in that moment, I was happy. And for now, that was enough.

The next day, he called me.

"Isn't it too long since we met?" he teased.

I laughed, shaking my head. "Yash, it was just the day before yesterday."

"Exactly," he said, as if proving a point.

I matched his playful tone. "Yaa, maybe we should meet… I think I might have forgotten how you look. Should we meet tomorrow?"

"Why wait till tomorrow?" he shot back without missing a beat. "What are you doing in another 20 minutes? Let's meet for a quick tea."

There was something about his spontaneity, the way he never overthought things, never hesitated. And without thinking too much myself, I said, "Yes."

I threw on a simple top and a comfortable pair of jeans, brushing my fingers through my hair as I checked my reflection. There was a nervous excitement bubbling inside me, an eagerness I didn't want to admit.

Stepping outside, I waited near my gate, my heart racing a little as I spotted his car pulling up. As soon as I slid into the passenger seat, that familiar scent hit me— His scent. The same intoxicating mix of cologne and something uniquely him.

His eyes, though slightly weary from a long workday, still held that quiet warmth, that pull I couldn't resist. The music was already on, loud, just the way he liked it. He was humming along, like it came as easy as breathing, and I let myself fall for his voice all over again.

It was just a five-minute drive, but I wished it were longer. We parked outside a nearby café, the kind of small, cozy place that felt untouched by the chaos of the outside world.

As we walked inside, he glanced at me. "Tea?" I scrunched my nose. "I'm more of a coffee person." He looked at me, pretending to be scandalized. "You don't drink tea?"

I laughed. "Nope. Never been a fan." He sighed dramatically. "That's it. We can't be friends anymore."

Rolling my eyes, I smirked. "Good thing we aren't just friends, then."

That got his attention. His smirk deepened, eyes locked onto mine. "Oh? And what are we?" I took a slow sip of my juice, pretending to think. "Hmm… I don't know. You tell me." He leaned back, studying me, as if trying to read between the lines. His fingers absentmindedly traced the rim of his cup.

"Something… interesting," he finally said, taking a slow sip of his tea.

Somewhere between one conversation and the next, in the middle of a random café, on a regular evening, my heart raced again.

It wasn't a grand moment. No dramatic confessions. No sweeping gestures. Just him.

Sitting across from me, his eyes half-lidded from exhaustion yet still so present—so undeniably there, like he always was.

We caught up, talking for about thirty minutes, letting the conversation flow with that same familiar ease it always had.

When he finally dropped me back home, he turned to me with that familiar look—the one that had become our quiet goodbye—and said, "Text me." And, as usual, I replied, "Message me once you reach home."

It had become our thing—unspoken, instinctive. A small routine that meant more than just words.

A few days later, I had plans to go out with my friends—clubbing, partying, letting loose for a night. During our regular call earlier that week, I casually mentioned it. That evening, before heading out, I messaged him,

Me: Can't talk today. Catch you later. He replied almost instantly.

Yash: Enjoy and have fun.

Simple. No questions. No hesitation. But then—right after, another message popped up.

Yash: Share your location when you leave the club.

I paused, reading his words again. He hadn't demanded it. He hadn't over-explained. Just a quiet insistence. A way of saying I care without making it a big deal. I had never had anyone ask me to share my location before. Not that I wasn't capable of handling myself—I always had been.

But deep down, I had secretly wanted someone to care. To make sure I was safe. To remind me, even in the smallest ways, that I mattered. And Yash had that in him. He was my safe place. It was late at night when I finally texted him.

Me: Starting from here. I shared my location, just as he had asked.

He didn't reply immediately, but I knew he saw it. And somehow, that was enough. When I reached home, I sent another message.

Me: I reached. His response came almost instantly.

Yash: Good. Now sleep. Good night.

Just four simple words. No unnecessary conversations. No long messages. But in that moment, they meant everything. It was as though he had been waiting, just to make sure I was safe. I stared at the screen, my fingers hovering over the keyboard.

This felt different. Good men are the most beautiful souls on earth. They might not always say the words. They might not always show grand gestures. But their actions—subtle, quiet, sincere—speak a thousand words.

And tonight, his actions told me everything I needed to know.

The next day at work, Tina narrowed her eyes at me the moment I walked in. "Okay, what's up with you?" she asked, crossing her arms. "New skincare routine?"

I just smiled, tucking my hair behind my ear. "Maybe!"

But deep down, I knew. It was him. It was the way he made me feel seen. The way he never had to ask for my attention, yet had all of it without trying. It was the way he cared—so quietly, so innately—that I hadn't realized how much I craved it.

Was this love? Or just attraction? Maybe it was nothing more than a beautiful distraction from the storm I had been going through. And yet—Distractions were supposed to be fleeting.

Temporary.

This didn't feel like that. This felt… different. Stronger. That realization sent a ripple of unease through me. I didn't want to fall in love. Love was complicated. Love meant vulnerability, expectations, and the fear of losing myself in someone else.

I had spent too long trying to keep my walls up— Was I really about to let them crumble so easily?

It wasn't the grand gestures.

It wasn't declarations of love.

It wasn't promises of forever.

It was him. Him, handing me the first bite of his meal, without fail. Always.

Even when I wasn't paying attention. Even when I wasn't expecting it.

I would be mid-conversation, distracted, my mind running elsewhere—

And then, his hand would appear in front of me, holding a spoonful, waiting.

No words. No need to ask. Just a quiet insistence that I take it.

I'd roll my eyes. "I can take my own food, you know." He'd smirk, ignoring me. "Eat." And I would.

Not because I had to, but because it felt like care wrapped in the simplest of gestures. The kind of care I wasn't used to. The kind I never had to ask for. The kind I never thought I needed—until him.

He wasn't the kind of man who made promises. He never told me he would quit smoking. He never pretended he would. He was honest, unapologetic, real. But he was also the man who always, without fail, made sure the smoke never reached me. He would exhale away from me, shift to the side, subtly adjust his stance— Not because I asked. Not because I made a fuss.

But because he noticed. Because he cared. Because even in the things he wouldn't change, he still made sure I was never uncomfortable.

He was never careless with me. Even in the smallest ways.

The way he always stood on the outer side of the road when we walked together, shielding me from passing traffic. The way he held my wrist lightly when crossing the street, just enough to guide, never to control. The way his arm would find its way around my back in a crowded place, keeping me close, a quiet assurance that I was safe. It was automatic. Unspoken. As though he'd always known how to be there for me—even before I knew I needed him to be.

And maybe… that was what shook me the most.

Because I had spent years guarding myself. Years being the one who took care of everything.

Of people.

Of emotions.

Of situations that demanded too much of me. I was used to carrying the weight.

And then there was him. Not asking me to let go, not trying to take over—

Just being there. Just treating me like someone worth being cared for.

Not a fragile girl.

Not someone to protect like I couldn't stand on my own.

But a woman. A queen. An equal, deserving of the same softness I had always given to others.

And I loved it. Every small moment. Every subconscious act of care. Every way he made me feel seen.

Because for the first time in my life— I didn't have to be strong for the both of us. I could just… be. And he would be there.

THE WEIGHT OF THE UNSPOKEN

Our messages and calls became a habit. Something I unconsciously looked forward to. Meeting for a quick tea wasn't a plan anymore; It was a pattern. Something familiar. Something I wasn't sure I could do without.

And that scared me. Because when you let yourself get used to someone… When you let them become part of your routine… When you start expecting their presence in your life…

It means they matter. And when someone matters, they have the power to hurt you. I wasn't sure I was ready for that.

I had been so consumed by him that I had completely forgotten about Urmi. Suddenly, a sharp twist of unease cut through me, pulling me back to reality. Should I tell her? Should I mention Yash?

A war raged inside me. I wasn't uncomfortable because of guilt— But because of doubt.

The memory of that video call still lingered in the back of my mind. Did something ever happen between them? Did she ever mean something to him?

More importantly— Did he ever mean something to her? A question I had to ask

That evening, I finally found the courage to ask Yash.

"Should we tell Urmi?" My voice was steady. My heart wasn't.

He barely hesitated. "Yeah, maybe we can call her for tea and spill."

That one simple response settled something inside me. If there had been anything between them, He wouldn't have been so open about it. He wouldn't suggest meeting her so casually.

And yet, even with that reassurance, I still felt the weight of my own doubts— Not about him. But about myself. Because no matter how much I fought it— One truth was becoming harder to ignore.

Yash wasn't just a distraction. And I wasn't sure I was ready for that.

As I navigated through the dense evening traffic, my mind drifted, tangled in thoughts I couldn't quite shake off. The city lights blurred past me, the hum of the engine a steady background noise, but my focus wasn't entirely on the road.

Yash's words from earlier echoed in my head.

"Yeah, maybe we can call her for tea and spill." It had sounded so casual, so easy for him. But for me? It wasn't. I wasn't sure if it was hesitation or fear,

But something about the idea of calling Urmi unsettled me. Would she care? Would she be surprised? Or worse— Would she already know?

Just then, his voice cut through my thoughts, pulling me back to the present. "Calling her?" he asked, his tone sharper than usual.

I blinked, gripping the steering wheel tighter. "What?" "You seem lost. Distracted. You were supposed to call her, right?"

His eyes were on me. Unreadable yet knowing. I exhaled slowly, the weight of the moment pressing down on me.

Was I making this more complicated than it needed to be? Or was there a reason I couldn't bring myself to dial her number?

I glanced at him, then back at the road. "Yeah... I will."

But even as I said it, I wasn't sure if I meant it. I kept my eyes on the road, my fingers gripping the steering wheel just a little tighter. The tension in the car was thick, pressing against my chest.

I had asked Yash to take my phone and dial Urmi's number— I wasn't ready to think too much about it.

She picked up after a few rings, her voice groggy.

"Hey, you busy?" I asked. "Just woke up from a nap," she mumbled.

I hesitated before saying, "I'm near your place. Want to grab a quick cup of tea?"

There was a brief pause. Then she replied, "Give me ten minutes."

She didn't ask who I was with. Maybe she assumed I was alone. Maybe she didn't think twice about it.

As we waited, my mind spiraled. How would she react when she saw Yash sitting next to me? Would she freeze? Would she turn around and walk away? Would she act like it was nothing?

And then— Before I could think any further, I saw her.

Urmi walked towards the car, her pace casual— Until she reached the front door and saw him. Her face shifted in an instant— Shock, surprise, maybe even something unreadable flickered through her eyes. She didn't say a word. She simply shut the front door and, without hesitation, Opened the back door instead, sliding in behind us.

Silence. The kind that stretches and suffocates.

Yash broke it first. "Hey," he said, his voice light, as if testing the waters.

Urmi responded in a soft tone, her voice cautious.

"Hi." And then, she turned her gaze to me.

"What is this?" she asked, her brows slightly furrowed. "You guys?" Her voice wasn't angry. It wasn't accusing. But it held something else— Curiosity, maybe. Or something deeper.

I inhaled, forcing a smile. "Yeah. Us."

Her eyes flickered between the both of us, searching for something—an explanation, a reason. I wasn't sure what to say. I wasn't even sure what this was myself.

The silence from earlier had stretched into something unspoken but present, lingering in the air as we walked into the small tea shop.

We ordered— Tea for them, coffee for me.

Urmi barely looked at me. Barely looked at Yash. But there was no tension, no visible discomfort— Just a quiet understanding that something had shifted.

As she sipped her tea, she turned to Yash. "Do you have a cigarette?"

He shook his head. "Don't have one on me."

Without another word, she stood. "I'll get one from outside."

Yash stood too, then turned to me, his voice low and even. "Come with me?"

I nodded, and just like that, the three of us stepped out—Urmi a few steps ahead, already on her mission.

And me, walking beside him. Too aware of the silence. Too aware of him.

The conversation was light—surface-level. Work. Random plans. Nothing too personal. I could tell she was still processing. Maybe she didn't want to ask. Maybe she didn't know how.

We finished our drinks, and as we walked back to the car, I turned to her. "I'll drop you home." Before she could respond, Yash spoke. "I'll drive."

I glanced at him, surprised. "You sure?" He nodded. "You had a long day. Just relax." I didn't argue. I handed him the keys, sliding into the passenger seat as Urmi got into the back.

As he drove, he was careful— Not in what he said, But in how he said it. He didn't declare anything, Didn't make it obvious, But he dropped hints— Little things only someone paying attention would catch.

I gave in. Not because I had to. But because, deep down, I wanted Urmi to know.

I don't even know what I was feeling—there was no clear label for it—but I wanted it to be known. That Yash and I were… something. Together, maybe not in the fully defined sense, but in a way that mattered. At least to me.

A casual mention of our usual tea runs. A small comment about something I had said the other day. The way his hand briefly brushed my knee when he shifted gears.

Urmi noticed. I could feel it. She didn't say anything. But she knew.

And maybe that was all I wanted—that quiet knowing. The unspoken acknowledgment that something had shifted. That something had begun.

Urmi called me the next day, her voice steady, but I could hear the weight beneath it—the kind of heaviness that lingers when something doesn't sit right.

"Can we meet?" she asked, not offering a reason, but we both knew why.

I hesitated before answering, my fingers tightening around the phone. I could sense the urgency in her voice, the unspoken weight of what she wasn't saying. But I wasn't ready—not yet.

"I'm swamped with work today," I said, keeping my tone light, casual. "But maybe later this week? Or over the weekend?"

A pause.

Urmi wasn't the kind of person who liked waiting. She thrived in the now, in spontaneity, in immediate answers. Delays, hesitations—they weren't her style. And yet, she didn't push.

"Okay," she said finally, her voice unreadable.

We hung up, but the silence she left behind stayed with me.

Two days passed. Then three.

The weight of Urmi's call lingered, pressing at the back of my mind like an unread message I couldn't bring myself to open. I had told myself I was busy—work, responsibilities, the usual excuses. But the truth was, I wasn't ready to face whatever conversation was waiting for me on the other side.

But I couldn't avoid it forever.

So, on the third evening, as I sat in my car, engine idling in the parking lot, I finally called her. She picked up almost instantly.

"Took you long enough," she said, her voice carrying an undertone I couldn't quite place. It wasn't anger. It wasn't impatience. It was something else—something subtle, yet impossible to ignore."

I forced a small chuckle. "I know, I know. Work's been crazy."

A pause. Then, "So, when are we meeting?"

No small talk. No pretenses. Straight to the point. I exhaled, drumming my fingers against the steering wheel. "Tomorrow? Same place?"

"Fine," she said. "8 PM."

Without hesitation, it was set. But as I ended the call, a strange feeling settled over me, gnawing at the edges of my thoughts. It was like something had shifted, and I wasn't sure I liked where it was going. Tomorrow, she'd ask. She'd want answers, clarity, explanations—things I wasn't sure I had.

And for the first time in a long time, I wasn't sure what I was going to say. Tell her I wasn't sure where this was going. Tell her that I wasn't thinking about the future, that I didn't know what this meant, that I didn't need to know—But I wanted to give it a try. Because he made me happy. And maybe for once, that was enough.

The bar was the same as always—dim lights casting warm shadows, the familiar hum of voices weaving into the background music, the quiet clink of ice against glass. A place where time moved slower, where conversations stretched without force.

But tonight, everything felt different. The weight in Urmi's voice, the concern in her eyes—it made the air feel heavier, like something unspoken was pressing down on us.

I took another slow sip of my drink, stalling. Letting the warmth of it settle before speaking.

"I don't know where this will take me," I admitted, more to myself than to her. My fingers traced the rim of my glass absentmindedly. "I'm not sure of this… whatever this is."

Urmi didn't interrupt. Didn't jump in with one of her usual quips or teasing remarks. She just watched me.

So I continued. "But he makes me happy, Urmi. Really happy." My voice softened, the words coming out quieter than I intended. "I feel… complete with him. Content. And I don't even want to name it."

Her expression didn't change, but I saw something shift in her eyes. A flicker of something—concern, hesitation. Maybe both.

And then she said it. "You know he's younger, right? Not just younger—young. They don't always take things seriously, not the way you do."

The words settled between us, quiet but sharp.

Of course I knew. I'd known from the start. But hearing it out loud, like a warning…

He might break you apart, she added, softer this time.

I swallowed, but my throat felt dry.

"Does that matter?" I asked, but it wasn't defiant. It wasn't a challenge. It was genuine. I was asking myself as much as I was asking her.

Urmi exhaled, shaking her head slightly, as if debating how much to say. And then, after a pause, she leaned in slightly, her voice lower now, more careful.

"Just think a million times before jumping into anything," she said. Her words weren't sharp. They weren't dismissive. They were laced with something real.

She wasn't warning me. She was pleading with me. I frowned. "Why do you say that?"

She hesitated, looking at me in a way that made my stomach twist before she finally spoke.

"Because I don't want you to get hurt."

Her words settled over me like a quiet truth. I opened my mouth to respond, but she wasn't done.

"You can see this, right?" she asked, her voice softer now, almost cautious. "That you're walking straight into a storm?"

I stilled. A storm. I didn't know what she meant.

Was she saying this was doomed? That it was reckless? That the end was inevitable? I stayed silent, waiting for her to continue.

"You'll never come back from this," she added, almost as if she already knew. As if she had already seen how this story would unfold before I had even admitted to myself that I was in it.

And for the first time, I realized—Urmi knew me better than I had given her credit for.

She knew this wasn't a passing phase. She knew this wasn't something I'd wake up from one day and shrug off like it never happened.

She knew. And maybe, deep down, I did too. And in the end, she just sighed, her expression softening.

"Just… be careful," she said, her voice quieter now, almost hesitant.

"I've never seen you like this before. You're all in— heart first, no guard. It's written all over your face. Just… don't lose yourself in him."

I nodded, not sure if I was agreeing or just acknowledging the weight of what she had said. But one thing was certain. It was too late. The storm wasn't something I was walking into. I was already drenched in it. But I wasn't sure if I believed myself.

A few days later, when I met Yash, I told him.

Told him I met Urmi.

Told him everything she had said.

Told him that I wasn't confused—at least, not about him.

We were sitting across from each other, in a café we had been to before. The kind of place where nothing needed to be explained, where familiarity settled between us like an old habit.

He leaned back in his chair, his usual relaxed self, arms crossed, watching me the way he always did—like he already knew what I was going to say before I even said it.

"I told Urmi that I like being around you," I said, stirring my coffee even though there was nothing left to stir.

He didn't respond immediately. Just tilted his head slightly, waiting.

"She asked me to think a million times before jumping into this," I continued, letting out a breathy laugh. "As if I don't already know what I'm doing."

His lips quirked into the barest hint of a smirk. "Do you?"

I looked at him. "I know one thing—I feel happy with you. I don't have to pretend. I don't have to think before I say something. I'm just... me."

Something flickered in his eyes, something quiet, something knowing.

"There's no doubt, Yash. Not for me. And I don't think for you either," I added, watching him carefully.

He nodded once, slow. "No. There's no uncertainty for me either."

Natural, undeniable, like it was the most obvious thing in the world.

There was no grand declaration, no need for unnecessary words. He knew what he felt. I knew what I felt. And we both knew that what we had was something.

"Then why are we talking about this?" he asked, tilting his head.

I exhaled, shaking my head. "Because I don't know where this will go. And I know you don't either."

He studied me for a beat, then leaned forward, resting his forearms on the table. "Does it have to go somewhere?" That made me pause.

He continued, voice calm, steady. "Can't we just live in the moment?"

I searched his face, looking for hesitation, for doubt.

But there was none.

Maybe that's what I liked about him. I overthought everything.

And he? He didn't overthink anything.

I nodded slowly. "Yeah. Maybe we can."

For a moment, I thought that was the end of the conversation. That we had settled whatever needed to be settled. But then—

He exhaled, tapping his fingers against the table. "I don't trust Urmi."

I blinked. "What?"

"I just don't," he said, gaze drifting past me for a second before returning, sharp and unwavering.

I studied him, trying to read between the lines. "What do you mean? You think she's lying to me?"

He shook his head. "No. It's my instinct."

I waited, expecting him to say more. To elaborate. To explain. But he didn't.

"She'll ruin things between us," he added instead, his voice steady.

I swallowed. "Why would she?"

His fingers stilled against the table, his expression unreadable. "Because that's how people are."

Like it was inevitable. Like the damage had already begun. Like it wasn't even up for discussion.

I studied him. "Was there ever anything between you and Urmi?" I needed to hear it. From him.

His answer came instantly. "No. Nothing." No hesitation. No flicker of doubt.

"She was just a neighbor, a friend. Nothing more, nothing less."

He didn't try to convince me. He didn't try to defend himself. He just… said it.

And that's what set him apart. He never felt the need to explain things in flowery words.

He never softened the truth to make it easier to hear. It is what it is.

"I just don't like the vibe she gives," he said simply.

That was it. No elaborate theories, no unnecessary warnings. Just his gut feeling. And he trusted it more than anything else.

But then— He did something that made me like him even more. He didn't ask me to choose. Didn't tell me to stay away from her.

He just shrugged, leaned back in his chair, and said,

"Anyway, it's your call. You've been friends with her for eight years. You should know what's best for you."

No ifs and buts. No pressure. Just clarity and I liked that about him. A man who wasn't afraid to say what he felt—but who also knew when to let me decide for myself.

Because that's the thing about Yash. He never forced anything. Never tried to control what wasn't his to control. He just existed in his truth.

And I was starting to realize— I liked existing in it too.

WHERE HUNGER MET ITS MATCH

It started as a simple plan

A text during the day. A casual decision—he would finish his cricket match and meet me at my place. Nothing serious. Nothing dramatic. No unnecessary buildup. Just us.

This wasn't just a meeting anymore. It felt like a slow-burning promise waiting to be fulfilled. The low hum of his car pulling up sent a pulse of anticipation through me. I had left the door unlocked.

When I heard it open, I turned— And there he was. The first glance that stole my breath.

Fresh from his match. His curls damp, falling over his forehead in messy perfection. His beard—sharp, rugged— making him look sharp in a way that didn't even try to be. His t-shirt clung to his chest, his shorts revealing strong legs, built for movement.

Everything about him screamed raw masculinity. Power. Confidence. But more than that— It was the way he looked at me. Like he had been waiting for this moment just as much as I had.

I sat in my recliner, pretending to be relaxed. Pretending that his presence didn't ignite something deep inside me. We talked. About random things. Things that didn't matter.

Filling the space between what we really wanted to say.

But I felt it.

The way he moved closer, inch by inch. The way his gaze held mine, steady, unblinking. Like he was memorizing me. Like he was waiting for me to feel what he already knew.

And then— Without a word, he stood in front of me. His presence towering, magnetic. His fingers reached down— Holding me. Pulling me.

In a heartbeat, the space between us vanished. I didn't hesitate. Not for a second.

I took his hints. Or maybe— Maybe I had been waiting for them all along.

His touch, my undoing. The first brush of his lips against my skin sent a rush through me. His neck. My shoulders. His hands moved with purpose, but his kisses— They were slow, deliberate. Like he was taking his time. Like he was savoring me.

And God— I couldn't resist. I didn't want to.

His fingers traced along my arms, leaving a burning trail in their wake.

His other hand found its way into my hair— Twirling it. Tugging it. Running his fingers through it like he had been waiting to do it forever.

I let out a shaky breath, leaning into his touch, my body reacting without hesitation.

He looked devastatingly handsome in that beard. I had always thought beards would be rough, scratchy, uncomfortable against my skin.

But his? It felt like second skin. Like something that had always belonged there.

I let my hands find him— Tracing the edge of his ears. Slipping under his t-shirt. His skin was fire beneath my fingertips. And when I ran my fingers along his back, he let out a deep, low moan— A sound I felt more than I heard. A sound that sent a shiver down my spine.

As our desires bloomed, time became a distant blur. Our bodies molded into each other, filling the gaps that once existed between us. Every touch, every breath, pulling us deeper into something we couldn't name.

Our feet brushed against each other— And suddenly, a soft gasp escaped me. His skin was warm. Mine was cold. The contrast sent a wave of electricity up my legs, making me more aware of every inch of him. He felt it too.

A knowing smirk played on his lips as he pressed his feet against mine again, teasing, testing, driving me insane. The simplest touch, the smallest movement, ignited something unbearable between us.

We weren't just kissing anymore. We were feeling, unraveling, discovering. Losing track of time.

I didn't know how long we stayed like that— Fingers tangled in each other's hair. Hands roaming, exploring. Our breaths syncing, our bodies speaking in ways our words never could.

The room around us faded. Time stretched, slow and intoxicating.

And I knew— This wasn't just physical. It was more.

It was consuming. A force greater than desire, deeper than need—something neither of us dared to name. Or maybe— It had already taken over.

And whether I was ready or not no longer mattered.

Because in that moment, I stopped questioning.

I stopped resisting.

I simply felt.

And for the first time in a long time— I let myself fall.

But love doesn't always arrive gently.

One evening, during our usual calls, his voice had a different edge to it. He wasn't teasing. He wasn't playful. He was pissed off. I could hear it in the way he exhaled, the way his words came sharper, clipped, laced with irritation.

"Something happened in my apartment today," he muttered. I sat up, immediately alert. "What happened?"

There was a long pause before he answered. "Urmi pissed me off"

I frowned. "What did she do?"

He took a breath, like he was still processing his own anger. "She went to my dad. Asked him to do something, without asking me first."

I waited.

"And I don't like that," he continued, his voice steady, but cold now. "I don't like when people cross lines. When they don't understand basic things."

He didn't have to say it outright— But I knew. Urmi had overstepped. And that was enough for him. Because when it comes to his family and his loved ones, Yash is different. He is protective. Possessive. It's one of the first things I had picked up about him—the way he doesn't just let people into his life. The way he keeps his circle small, his trust even smaller. And once someone crosses a line? That's it.

No second chances. No explanations. No apologies. Just distance.

And so, he simply said,

"That's it. I'm blocking her. I don't want to deal with people who can't understand basic things."

Without a second thought, no hesitation, no looking back. The clarity I admired quiet but unwavering. Given that he was so much younger than me, I found myself liking this about him. His clarity. His decisiveness. The way he didn't overthink things the way I did.

For him, things were black and white— Either you understand boundaries, or you don't. Either you respect him, or you don't. Either you belong in his life, or you don't. It was so simple for him.

And maybe, deep down, I envied that. Because I was the opposite. I carried doubt. I questioned my own feelings. I let people stay longer than they should.

But Yash? He didn't. And for some reason, I liked that about him. I didn't argue.

Didn't try to make him see it differently. Didn't try to soften his decision. Because that wasn't my place.

So instead, I simply said, "It's okay. If you don't like her, that's your call."

And I meant it.

"It's not going to affect anything between us." And maybe— Maybe that was the first time I realized something.

Something Urmi had said to me that night over drinks. He is younger than you- young. And yet— Somehow, he was the one who had it all figured out. While I was still trying to find my own clarity.

Life had taken over.

Work, family, responsibilities—each demanding more than I could possibly give, each pulling me in different directions. It wasn't intentional, this drifting apart. It wasn't because we wanted less of each other. It was just reality.

The way we used to fold into each other's lives had turned into something sporadic, fleeting—our meets reduced to barely twice or thrice a month. Time, once abundant, had become a luxury we couldn't afford.

And yet, despite the distance, despite the missed calls and unread texts, we still found ways to exist in each other's world.

Not through late-night conversations that stretched till dawn. Not through passionate confessions or dramatic declarations. Not even through the kind of messages that spelled out exactly what we meant.

But through something as simple as reels on Instagram. A tap. A forward. A notification.

"Yash sent you a reel."

At first, I never understood it—the whole thing about sending reels. What was the point? Why not just say something instead?

But then, I thought about it. I sent reels to my best friends, didn't I? The funny ones, the relatable ones, the ones that made me pause and think, this reminds me of them. It was simple, reflexive—like muscle memory wrapped in affection. A tiny gesture that said, I saw this and thought of you.

So why couldn't love be expressed like this? Why couldn't a simple reel mean I miss you? Or I care about you? Or I wish you were here? Because that's what it was, wasn't it?

A romantic line from a movie, sent without explanation. A song that carried unspoken words. A stupid joke that made no sense but still made me smile. A five-second clip of something completely random, yet in that very moment, I knew— He was thinking of me.

Maybe it wasn't a grand gesture. Maybe it wasn't poetry or love letters or flowers at my doorstep.

But every time my phone buzzed, every time his name lit up on my screen, it felt warm. Familiar. Like a quiet reassurance that no matter how busy life got, no matter how long it had been since we last saw each other— He was still there. We were still here.

I wasn't sure. I didn't know if this was love or just a beautiful habit that I wasn't ready to break.

But I knew this— It made me happy. And for now, that was enough.

Yash never explicitly asked for things. He wasn't the kind of man who hinted at gifts or dropped subtle suggestions about what he wanted. But there were moments—small, fleeting ones—where his desires revealed themselves in the midst of casual conversations.

One of those moments came when we were talking about exhaustion. About work stretching too long, about cricket matches draining the last bit of energy he had left, about the relentless grind of gym sessions that pushed his body to its limit.

I remembered how often he had said it. "Wish someone would give me a massage."

It wasn't a serious request. More of a passing remark, something he never dwelled on. But I had caught it. And though I never said anything, it stayed with me.

I had never given him a massage before. Sure, I had run my fingers through his hair, massaged his scalp absentmindedly while we sat together, letting the silence between us settle into something easy. I had traced circles on his back when he leaned against me after a long day. But an actual massage? A real, proper, take-away-the-fatigue kind of massage? Never.

And yet, the way he had said it—wish someone would give me a massage—it had always carried a weight of longing, like something he truly craved but never asked for.

So when his birthday was nearing, and I found myself searching for something to gift him, nothing felt right.

We weren't together in the conventional sense. No labels. No definitions. We had an understanding, a connection, an us that couldn't be neatly boxed into words. And because of that, traditional gifts didn't feel appropriate.

A watch? Too predictable. Clothes? Too impersonal. Something sentimental? Too much.

I wanted something that wasn't just a gift, but an experience. Something that would bring him actual joy.

And then, suddenly, I knew exactly what to get him. A body massage voucher.

It was the perfect mix of thoughtful and practical—something he truly needed but would never get for himself. Something that showed I had been paying attention. Something that would take away his stress, his exhaustion, even if just for an hour.

I booked it immediately. A full-body deep tissue massage at a well-rated spa. The kind that would work out the knots in his muscles, that would leave him feeling lighter, rejuvenated.

And then, I waited.

The morning of his birthday, I sent him a message: "Check your WhatsApp."

Seconds later, the blue ticks appeared.

And then—

Yash: What's this?

Me: "Your birthday gift. Happy birthday, idiot."

I stared at my screen, waiting for a reaction.

One minute. Two minutes. No reply.

And then—

Yash: You're crazy. I can't believe you actually did this. You're insane.

I laughed to myself, imagining the look on his face.

Me: You always say you need a massage. Thought I'd make sure you get one.

Yash: This is the most thoughtful gift I've ever gotten. I swear. Who even thinks of gifting a massage?

I could almost hear the disbelief in his voice.

It wasn't flashy. It wasn't expensive. But it was him— it was something I knew he needed, even if he had never outright asked for it.

His next message was quieter.

Yash: I really, really love this. Thank you.

Something about those words made my chest tighten, my heart do a slow, quiet flip. This wasn't just about a gift. This was about knowing him.

Knowing that he would never book a massage for himself. Knowing that he would never prioritize his own rest, his own care. Knowing that even though he carried exhaustion like second skin, he would never admit how much he needed a break.

But I knew. I always knew.

A few days later, he finally redeemed the voucher.

Yash: Just got done.

Me: And?

Yash: I feel like a new man. Holy shit. This was the best idea ever. I never knew I needed this so badly.

I smiled at my phone.

Me: Told you.

Yash: You're unreal, you know that? I can't get over the fact that you thought of this.

Me: Yeah, yeah. Just admit I'm the best.

Yash: You already know it.

For the rest of the night, his messages were different. Softer. Warmer. As if something had shifted.

It wasn't just the relaxation. It wasn't just the fact that his body finally felt loose, his muscles no longer aching. It was the feeling of being cared for.

I had given him a moment of peace. A break from the weight of the world. And somehow, in a way I never expected, that meant everything. That night, before we both fell into silence, he sent one last message.

Yash: No one's ever done something like this for me before.

And maybe that was the real gift. Not just the massage. Not just the hour of relaxation.

But the knowing. The understanding that someone saw him—not just as a man who could handle everything, who carried the world without complaining—but as someone who deserved to be taken care of too.

And that? That was priceless.

THE BEAUTY IN THE ORDINARY

Sometimes, we argued. Not over big things. But over small, stupid things that somehow still mattered. A message left unread. A reply that came too late.

Sometimes, over my partying— The nights out, the people, the guy I happened to talk to at some club. It wasn't about trust. Not really. It was him wanting to be a part of my world, even when he wasn't there.

I didn't think much of it. I wasn't someone who explained herself to anyone. But with him— I found myself doing it. Not because I had to, But because I wanted to. Because in some way, I liked his attention on me. I liked the way he asked. I liked his possessiveness.

Maybe because I had never been asked before. Maybe because I was craving that attention— The kind that made me feel like I was someone to be cared for.

The comfort in the chaos even when we fought, even when I was frustrated with him, with myself, with us— I still felt comfortable around him.

That was the difference. I didn't have to filter myself. I didn't have to overthink how I spoke, how I reacted. With him, I could just be. No artificial charm. No exhausting effort to be likable, agreeable, perfect. Just me.

And maybe— Maybe that's what made it so hard to define what this was. Because I wasn't sure if it was love. But I was sure— I hadn't felt like this before.

Distance had never been an issue. Not with him. It didn't matter where he was, how far—if he wanted to see me, if I wanted to see him, I would be there.

There was never hesitation, never a second thought. I would grab my car keys, dial his number, and say, "I'm coming."

He never made me question if I should come. He never made me feel like I was going out of my way. It was always easy.

"I'm leaving now." "Okay, drive safe."

And he never stopped me. He never said, Don't take the trouble. He never made excuses. He never told me it wasn't necessary.

Because he knew. He knew I wanted to. He knew I didn't see it as a chore. He knew that picking him up wasn't just about the drive—it was about something more.

It was about the way he made me feel. Wanted. Desired. Not just for stolen moments, not just for fleeting passion, but for his time.

He didn't say it in words, but I felt it— in the way he would be waiting for me, the way he would slide into the passenger seat with that familiar smirk, the way his eyes would soften when he looked at me, like he had been waiting for this exact moment all day.

I loved watching him get into my car. The way he made himself comfortable instantly, stretching his legs, his fingers moving to adjust the AC, the music—as if he belonged there. And in a way, he did.

My car, my space, it felt different with him in it. It wasn't just mine anymore.

It was ours. He would pull his seat back, lean into the headrest, close his eyes for a second—just a second—before glancing at me with a lazy smile.

"Tired?" I would ask. He would shrug. "Not anymore." And that? That was enough.

Sometimes, our drives stretched longer than planned. Sometimes, we didn't go anywhere at all. We would just sit there, parked in some quiet lane, lost in conversation.

He would fidget with my bracelet, intertwine his fingers with mine absentmindedly, tap his fingers on the dashboard to the beat of the song playing. Sometimes, he would just watch me. His gaze, steady, intent. Like he was trying to memorize me. Like he was drinking me in, taking note of the way the streetlights reflected on my skin, the way my hair fell over my shoulder.

And sometimes, in the middle of all that stillness, he would do something so simple, so intimate—he would pull my hand to his lips, press a slow kiss against my palm, then continue talking as if nothing happened.

And God, how was I supposed to breathe after that? There was no hesitation in what we had. No questions. No doubt. Just an understanding that this was what we did. Because he was mine. Even if we never said it. Even if the world didn't know it. He was mine. And I was his. For as long as time allowed.

One night, he called me over to his place. No special occasion. No elaborate plan. Just us.

We sat there, wrapped in the kind of comfort that doesn't need words—listening to music, talking about his early life, his stories, his past. It was simple.

But it felt like something I'd want to bottle up forever. Because there's something about a man who is gentle. A man who is soft, yet strong. A man who respects you— not just in grand moments, but in the quiet, everyday ones.

Yash was that. And every time I met him, I found myself mesmerized all over again.

There's something about late night cravings. A 2 AM craving that felt like more. It was late. Past 2 AM. Most nights, this is when exhaustion would creep in, when conversations would start fading into drowsy silence. But not with him.

He was hungry. A craving for Subway, of all things. I laughed when he said it, but we ordered anyway. And when it arrived, when he unwrapped the sandwich like it was some masterpiece, when he took that first bite and sighed in satisfaction— 'I couldn't stop watching him. Not because of what he was eating. But because of how he was eating.

He does everything with his whole heart— When he works, he gives his all. When he plays, he loses himself in the game. And when he eats? He truly enjoys it. No distractions. No scrolling on his phone. Just him, savoring every bite, completely in the moment.

I absolutely loved watching him eat. It was so normal, so routine—something anyone could overlook. And yet, somehow, I felt lucky to witness it. Because life isn't made up of grand romantic gestures, candlelit dinners, or dramatic confessions. It's made up of nights like this. A craving at 2 AM. A man who eats like he truly enjoys his food. A moment so unremarkable, yet unforgettable.

And as I sat there, watching him, listening to him go on about how tasty it was, how satiating it felt— I realized something. Sometimes, love isn't a big declaration. Sometimes, it's just watching someone be themselves. And realizing you wouldn't want to be anywhere else.

We were drifting—somewhere between sleep and wakefulness. The kind of quiet exhaustion that comes after hours of talking, listening to music, and that perfect late-night Subway meal.

Everything felt complete. There was nothing left to say, nothing left to do. Just the warmth of him pulling me into his arms, his heartbeat steady against mine. I felt safe. I felt at home. And just as I was slipping into sleep, I heard it.

"I love you." His voice was soft, almost like he hadn't planned to say it.

But it was there now, lingering in the space between us. And suddenly—time froze. My heart stopped. I didn't know what to say. I didn't know how to react. I just... froze. And in that moment, instead of answering, instead of letting him see the storm inside me— I pretended to be asleep.

I felt his breath still against my hair, his arms still wrapped around me, waiting for something. But I couldn't give it to him. Not because I didn't want to. But because I was scared. The fear that held me back.

Maybe it was the fear of losing someone to love. Maybe it was the fear of losing myself to love. I had been hurt before. I had spent days, nights, weeks crying over someone who never looked back. I had given my heart away too easily once, and it was taken for granted.

And that fear? It was still there. Still heavy on my chest, still whispering—"Don't fall. Don't trust. Don't say it back."

But deep inside— I wanted to scream. I wanted to say it back with everything inside me. I wanted to tell him that I too loved him, That he made me feel things I didn't think I could feel again. That this was real, and I wasn't just in it for the moment.

But I didn't have the courage to utter a single word. So I let the silence speak for me. I let the darkness swallow my truth. And I just lay there, eyes shut, heart pounding, afraid of the one thing I wanted the most.

The next morning, I left from his place, the warmth of his embrace still lingering on my skin. His hugs were always the same—strong, steady, comforting. Like a silent promise that even in uncertainty, I was safe with him.

But we didn't discuss last night's awkwardness. Didn't bring up the three words he whispered into the dark. We just let it be. A quick kiss, soft and familiar.

And then, as always— "Drop a message once you reach home."

As I drove back home, the city still quiet in the early morning haze, my thoughts spiraled in circles. What am I doing? Am I going to get hurt?

We, as humans, have always complicated relationships so much. We tiptoe around emotions, analyzing, doubting, holding back— All because we are too scared to deal with people, too scared to deal with feelings. And in that fear, we end up lonely. We end up losing people who actually love us.

Did he love me? Or was it just care? I didn't know if Yash actually loved me. But I knew one thing— He cared for me. Deeply.

He liked it when he spent time with me. He liked us. And Yash wasn't difficult to understand. He didn't hide behind mixed signals or complicated emotions. He was direct. Clear. Honest.

Maybe the real issue was— It wasn't difficult to understand him. It was difficult to understand myself. The weight of overthinking.

At work, I felt gloomy. Lost in my own head, drifting through tasks I barely registered. Tina noticed instantly. She always did. She didn't push, didn't demand answers. She simply asked, "What is it that's bothering you?"

I didn't tell her everything. But she knew. She knew about my fear. My insecurities. She knew that no matter how strong I pretended to be, love was my greatest fear.

But Tina wasn't the kind of friend who pried. She was the kind who just stayed. Who let you feel what you needed to feel.

And when I finally looked at her, she simply said— "I don't know why you're so afraid. I don't know what your insecurities are. But why can't you just go with the flow?" The words hit me like a punch to the gut.

Because wasn't that exactly what I always told her? "Go with the flow." I had preached it so easily. But when it came to my own life— I couldn't do it. I couldn't just let go, just feel, just be.

And that was the problem. I was so scared of what I couldn't control— That I was keeping myself from something that actually made me happy. But in doing that, I was shutting the door on the very things that made life unpredictable, messy—and beautiful.

Fights were inevitable. We had argued before—small disagreements, fleeting moments of frustration that disappeared as quickly as they came. But this? This was different. This was the first time we fought and didn't speak for more than a day.

A full day. And then some more. It was strange, unsettling, and I hated every second of it. The fight that started and it wasn't even a big deal. But isn't that how the worst fights begin? With something small, seemingly insignificant, until it snowballs into something bigger than either of us intended? Maybe I said too much. Maybe he didn't say enough.

All I remember is him saying, "I just need space." And that was it. No anger. No shouting. No storm of words left hanging between us. Just silence. A cold, unsettling silence that settled deep in my chest, leaving behind an ache I didn't know how to shake off. The silence that hurt like hell.

He was traveling to his hometown anyway. Maybe it was a good timing. Maybe it was just an excuse. Either way, we agreed. We would give each other the space we needed.

Let's agree—Relationships are hard. Balancing expectations, work, life, emotions—it's exhausting. And sometimes, space is necessary. But necessary or not, it hurt like hell.

I didn't know what was worse— The distance itself, Or the way it settled so easily between us, like it had always been there, waiting.

There was no good morning text. No midday check-in. No random memes or reels shared in between work breaks. Just an empty phone screen. And God, how I hated it. I tried to distract myself—throwing myself into work, drowning in deadlines, telling myself, This is fine. This is needed.

But who was I kidding? It wasn't fine. I wasn't fine. I missed him. I missed his voice. I missed us. But I accepted it. I did what needed to be done. I gave him the space he asked for, even though it was the last thing I wanted to do.

After 36 long, unbearable hours, my phone finally buzzed.

Yash.

My fingers trembled as I unlocked my phone, my heart hammering in my chest. The message was simple. "I want to talk to you." "I missed you." In that moment, the silence was shattered, sharp and unyielding, breaking the fragile stillness between us. Like a floodgate bursting open, every emotion I had been pushing down rushed back all at once.

I should have made him wait. I should have held my ground. I should have pretended I wasn't affected, wasn't aching for him the way I was. But instead, I gave in. I texted back. I called.

And the moment I heard his voice— I broke. I wanted to be mad. I wanted to ask why did you shut me out? But all I could manage was, "I missed you too."

Somewhere between the apologies and soft sighs, I realized— It was my fault. I had overreacted, let my insecurities get the best of me. So I swallowed my pride and said it. "I'm sorry."

And his response? It was immediate. "It's okay. I love you. So simple. So heartbreakingly easy. Like he didn't realize how much I needed to hear it. Like he had been waiting to say it again. Like it wasn't even a question in his mind.

And yet— I still couldn't say it back. Because love still scared me. Because love still meant expectations, and promises, and risk. Because I had given my heart away once before, and I wasn't sure if I could survive losing it again.

And then—He said something that shook me to my core. "I want us to be forever." "I don't know how, or what that looks like. But whatever this is—I don't want it to end."

My breath caught in my throat. Forever? Forever had never been a word I allowed myself to believe in. Forever meant certainty. Forever meant commitment. Forever meant falling completely, without a safety net. And I wasn't sure I was ready for that.

The confession that left me speechless, not a name, not a definition—Just us.

He wasn't talking about labels, or commitments, or the kind of promises people make when they're caught in the moment. He was talking about us. The feeling. The unspoken truth.

That we had different lives, different routines, different responsibilities. That there was no certainty in the future. That we didn't need to define what we were. We just knew we felt good together. And that was enough. He wasn't asking me for a promise. He wasn't asking me for an answer.

He was just saying— "I want this. Whatever this is. And I don't want to lose it."

And me? I felt the same. I wanted him. I wanted this. I wanted to hold onto this feeling for as long as I could. But I was still too scared to say it out loud. So I gave him the only answer I could.

"Yes. As long as we can." And for now— That was enough.

Each passing day, something shifted inside me. It wasn't sudden. It wasn't dramatic. But it was there— growing, unfolding, becoming impossible to ignore. This wasn't just a distraction. Not a temporary escape from my otherwise predictable life. Not a passing phase that would fade as quickly as it came.

It was love. And yet—I wasn't admitting it. Not to him. Not even to myself.

Because love? Love meant vulnerability. Love meant risk. Love meant giving someone the power to break you and trusting them not to. And that terrified me. The fear that wouldn't let me breathe.

With every moment we spent together, every glance that lingered a second too long, every quiet confession he made, a new fear began to settle inside me. What if one day, this all shatters? What if we have to part ways? What if this wasn't forever, after all? What if one morning, I wake up, and he's just gone?

His absence wouldn't just be silence. It wouldn't just be an empty space on my phone, or a missing name in my notifications. It would be a void so deep, I wouldn't know how to fill it. Because he wasn't just someone I cared for. He wasn't just someone I liked spending time with. He had become a part of me. A part of my routine, my thoughts, my world.

Losing him wouldn't just be painful. It would be unbearable. And yet, I wasn't stopping myself. Because even though the fear was real, Even though I knew this could end one day, Even though I knew I might lose him just as suddenly as I found him— I wanted him anyway. Even if it meant breaking my own heart in the process.

CAUGHT BETWEEN TWO WORLDS

It started as a simple call—one of those routine conversations we had in between our busy lives. I was in the middle of wrapping up my day when his name flashed on my screen.

"Can we meet?"

His voice was casual, but something about the way he asked made me pause for a second. It wasn't just a spontaneous plan. It was the kind of ask that meant, I just want to be with you for a while.

I glanced at the time. It was already late evening. A long day had drained me, but something in me instantly said yes.

"Yeah… maybe a quick dinner?" I suggested.

"Okay," he agreed. "You decide."

I rolled my eyes. Why was he always like this? "No, you decide."

"I didn't get time to think about it," he admitted. "I'll figure something out when you get here."

Typical. I sighed but smiled to myself. "Fine, I'll pick you up in a bit." As I neared his office, I called him. "Come down, I'm here."

A few minutes later, he appeared. His hair slightly ruffled, shirt sleeves rolled up to his elbows, a little rumpled, a little worn out, and still annoyingly good at pulling it off. He slid into the passenger seat, stretching a little before settling in.

"Where to?" I asked. He blinked. "Uhh… I didn't get time to check any place."

I shot him a look. "Yash, I'm famished. And you didn't even decide?" I wasn't seriously annoyed, but hunger was making me impatient. He smirked, unfazed. "Let's pull over somewhere, have a juice while we decide?" I sighed. "Fine."

We stopped at a small juice shop nearby. The kind of place where the lights were too bright, the menu too long, and the choices never-ending. I took a sip of my fresh orange juice while he watched me, his fingers tapping idly against the glass.

"Feeling better?" he teased.

I rolled my eyes, but the irritation had already melted away. After much back-and-forth, we settled on a nearby barbecue place. It wasn't fancy, but it had the best grilled meat and kebabs.

The moment the food arrived, we ate like we hadn't eaten in days. The delicious smoky flavors, the spice, the way the meat melted in our mouths—it was comfort food at its finest.

We talked. About work. About random things. About nothing at all. And it felt good. Conversations with him never felt forced. They unfolded in that quiet, familiar way where silence felt just as welcome as words. Like we were two people who just existed in the same world, sharing small slices of life in between everything else.

After dinner, he leaned back in his chair, looking absolutely stuffed. "I overate," he groaned. I laughed. "You always do."

He stretched, running a hand through his hair. "I need a smoke."

I raised an eyebrow. "What if I start smoking?"

He looked at me, amused, before letting out a soft laugh. "You? Never."

He knew me too well. And just like always, when he lit his cigarette, he turned his body slightly—ensuring the smoke drifted away from me, shielding me from it like he always did. Small things. Unspoken things. Things that made me realize he cared. I liked that he never made fake promises. Never said, I'll quit for you. He was real. Honest. Just him.

We got back in the car, and I started driving towards his place. He slouched into the seat, half-asleep, the exhaustion from the long day finally catching up to him.

I glanced at him and smiled. "Sleepy?"

"Hmm," he muttered, eyes barely open. "I overate. My body's shutting down."

"Sleep, then." I said.

He hummed in response, his voice laced with drowsiness. For the rest of the drive, he remained quiet, head tilted slightly toward the window, completely at ease, eyes half-closed, but his hands still held mine. He never let go.

I liked that. Him holding my hand. Just that.

And I... I just watched him whenever I could, wondering how someone could look so peaceful even in a state of exhaustion.

When we reached his place, I stopped the car. "Alright, sleepyhead. Get out." He opened his eyes slightly, smirking. "Come inside." I shook my head. "Naah, I should head home."

"Just for a while," he said, voice soft but sure.

I hesitated. And then, I agreed. Just for a while.

The apartment was dimly lit, the air slightly cooler than outside. The moment we entered, he kicked off his shoes, stretched lazily, and fell onto the bed. I followed, standing there for a beat, suddenly aware of the dress I was in—not exactly something I wanted to stay in.

He noticed. "Here," he said, tossing me one of his t-shirts from the chair. "You'll be more comfortable."

Without a word, I slipped it on right there, letting the dress fall to the floor in a soft rustle. He didn't stare. He just smiled, like it was the most normal thing in the world. I hopped onto the bed next to him, his t-shirt drowning me slightly, smelling faintly of him.

It was quiet. No passion. No urgency. Just the kind of silence that didn't need to be filled. He reached for my hand, intertwining his fingers with mine. "This feels nice."

I didn't answer. Just squeezed his hand lightly. After a while, he murmured, "Set an alarm, or you'll be late tomorrow."

I did as he said, setting my phone on the nightstand. Then, without even thinking, I curled up next to him. His warmth seeped into my skin, his steady breathing settling something restless inside me. Without a word, we drifted into sleep.

The alarm buzzed, pulling me from the depths of sleep. For a moment, I didn't move. Didn't want to. The bed was warm, his presence beside me a comfort I didn't want to let go of. He stirred beside me, mumbling something incoherent before pulling me closer.

"Do you really have to go?" he murmured, voice thick with sleep. I sighed. "Yeah." He exhaled slowly, like he didn't want this moment to end.

I pulled myself away gently, sitting up and rubbing my eyes. He watched me, still half-asleep, propping himself up on one elbow.

"Text me when you reach?" I smiled. "Always."

As I stepped out into the early morning air, the city still wrapped in its last moments of sleep, I carried the warmth of the night with me.

Sometimes, love—or whatever this was—wasn't about grand gestures. It was about quiet moments. Shared meals. A protective glance. A night spent wrapped in nothing but silence and warmth. It was about being with each other, in peace, in stillness. And sometimes, that was enough.

Life had pulled us apart again. Same old work. Responsibilities. Commitments. We met less. Spoke less. But I didn't mind—not too much.

Because we had a plan. Because we were finally meeting after weeks. I had spent the whole day counting down the hours. The excitement buzzing in my chest, the thought of seeing him after so long warming every inch of me.

And then— One phone call changed everything. The news that shattered my excitement "I have a terrible pain in my back." His voice was strained, weak. Something inside me twisted in worry.

"Did you see a doctor?" "Yeah… I'll be fine," he assured me. But minutes later— A text lit up my screen. "I've been admitted to the hospital."

My heart stopped. My hands trembled as I stared at the message, reading it over and over, as if it would change.

Hospital? How did things escalate this fast? How was I not there? How could I do nothing but wait for updates? I wanted to see him. To hold his hand, to tell him it would be okay. But all I could do was sit with my worry, my heart racing, my mind filled with a thousand 'what-ifs.'

I prayed. Day and night. Silently. Desperately. Because what else could I do? The ache of separation, a quiet longing that lingers in the spaces between us.

Few days later, he told me he was going to his hometown for three months. Three. Whole. Months.

The words felt like a punch to my chest. I barely had time to process his illness, and now, he was leaving? How was I supposed to go three months without seeing him? And more than that—how would we even talk?

With his family around him all the time, with responsibilities pulling him in every direction, would we even have time for each other? Would he forget me? Would we fade away— in the quietest of ways?

But then, reality crashed in. What was I even expecting? This was bound to happen. He had his own life. I had mine. Forever was never a thing between us. We both knew it. But knowing didn't make it hurt any less.

And yet— Even in the middle of everything, he still found a way. He still chose me. Even when he was surrounded by family, buried under obligations, caught up in his world— He made time. Video calls became our thing.

Whenever he could steal a moment, he would sneak away and call me. Sometimes for just two minutes.

Sometimes for twenty. But every single time— It made me feel wanted. It made me feel chosen.

Because the truth about men? Real men don't ignore. It's simple for them. They are either there, or they're not. And Yash? He was there. Even in the smallest ways.

Even in stolen moments. Even when it wasn't easy. And for the first time in a long time, I realized— Maybe this was real. Maybe this was what it felt like to be with someone who truly cared.

Maybe… Maybe I was falling deeper than I ever meant to. But whatever it was—I decided to just go with the flow.

The weight of helplessness sat heavy on my chest, pressing into me with every passing day that Yash was away, recovering from his back injury. I had never felt this kind of restlessness before—this constant need to do something, anything, to make things better. But what could I do? I couldn't be there, couldn't ease his pain, couldn't take away the discomfort.

And so, almost instinctively, I decided—I would go to the temple.

I would pray for him.

I would offer something in his name.

I would find a way, however small, to feel like I was helping.

As I drove through the quiet streets, the weight of my own actions began to settle in. The familiar hum of the city blurred into the background as my thoughts swirled.

Why was I doing this? It wasn't like me.

I had never done this for anyone.

Not for my past relationships, not for friends, not even for myself.

But for him?

For him, I would go.

For him, I wanted to.

I just wanted him to heal. I just wanted him back on his feet. Back to being the man who never sat still, the man who was always moving, always alive with energy. I wanted him whole again. And if that meant seeking something beyond my control, placing my faith somewhere I never had before—then so be it.

Because when it came to him, logic didn't matter. Only the feeling did.

And right now, the feeling was undeniable. Because, after all, when everything else fails—when logic, control, and even the weight of our own emotions aren't enough— it's God we turn to. When helplessness takes over, when the ache of wanting but not being able to do anything consumes us, we surrender. We offer prayers, whispered in desperation, sent out into the universe with nothing but hope.

And that's what I was doing. I wasn't someone who relied on faith. I had always believed in action, in fixing things with my own hands, in taking charge rather than waiting for miracles. But this—this was different.

Because I couldn't fix this. I couldn't take his pain away. I couldn't be there. All I had were my prayers, my silent offerings, my quiet plea for him to heal.

And so, I drove toward the temple, seeking something I had never sought before.

Because when love—or whatever this was—collides with helplessness, even the strongest of us find ourselves looking up, hoping that somewhere, someone is listening.

I had to be practical. But in that moment life didn't pause just because he was away.

I had my world here. My routine. My people. I went out with my friends. I laughed, I drank, I tried to live as if nothing had changed. But it had. I felt it in the way I checked my phone more often than usual.

In the way my heart anticipated his name lighting up my screen. In the way every conversation somehow circled back to him. And no matter where I was, or who I was with— A part of me was always with him.

The little things that kept us connected. Even from miles away, we still had our thing. Sometimes, when I was out, I would text him, teasing him— "ZEE is missing you."

And his reply would always be the same— A simple smile. But behind that smile, I knew the truth. I knew he never liked it when I mentioned Urmi. Not even a little. He would never tell me not to meet her. He wasn't that kind of man. He was too secure, too self-aware to be controlling.

But I could feel it— In the way his responses turned shorter. In the way his teasing suddenly faded. In the way he would change the topic, nudging the conversation in a different direction before I even realized it. It was subtle. But it was there. His silence said more than words ever could.

And me? I was caught between two worlds. Between friendship, the kind that had stood by me for years, through heartbreaks, through chaos, through life itself. Torn between loyalty and love.

And a man who made me feel something I had never felt before. Whole. Complete. Like I belonged somewhere—with him. And yet, I couldn't walk away from either. I couldn't abandon a friendship that had been a constant.

But I also couldn't ignore the pull of the man who had become my peace. And maybe— Maybe I should have listened to his instincts. Because if there was one thing I knew about him, it was this— His intuition was never wrong.

And yet, I held on to both, trying to balance the past and the present, comfort and something dangerously close to love. But balance? It never lasts forever.

I had been laughing just minutes ago. A carefree day with friends, conversations flowing, the world feeling light for once. I messaged him that I reached back home and I had a lovely time.

And then—his text. "I've been meaning to tell you something for a while now." But don't be mad!

The air shifted. I frowned at my screen, rereading his words, a strange sense of unease creeping up my spine. What was it that he wanted to say? And why now?

"Tell me," I typed back. "But if it's something that'll make me mad, I will be mad."

I meant it playfully. A teasing response, the way I always was with him. Because this was Yash—he knew me, he knew my temperament, and yet, he was never scared to say things as they were.

"Promise me you won't react first."

My fingers hesitated over the keyboard. The unease solidified into something real, tangible. "Just say it, Yash."

All at once, the words appeared on my screen—words that shouldn't have mattered, but somehow, they broke through a quiet wall inside me, leaving me unsure of what to feel next.

"There's this girl. I like her a lot. And I think she likes me too."

The world tilted. For a split second, everything blurred. The sound of people around me faded into a dull hum, the lights in the room felt too bright, too intrusive. I blinked at the screen, my breath catching, my chest tightening with a kind of pain I wasn't prepared for.

No. No, this had to be one of his pranks.

"Haha. Very funny, Yash. Now tell me what it really is."

But the next text— "I'm serious."

That was the moment the ground beneath me cracked open. I swallowed, but my throat felt tight, like something was lodged there. My fingers trembled slightly as I gripped my phone.

This couldn't be real. Yash—the one who made me believe in something beyond just responsibility, the one who had always been mine in a way that defied logic— was saying he liked someone else?

I didn't respond. I couldn't.

I excused myself, made my way to the washroom, locked the door behind me, and stared at my own reflection. My face was unreadable, but my eyes—God, my eyes—held the storm I was barely containing.

And then, the tears came. Silent, burning, endless.

The phone buzzed again. And again. Messages piling up. But I couldn't bring myself to read them. I couldn't bring myself to face it.

Then his call. I let it ring. Another one. I let it ring again. And then—his text.

"We are not even in the same city to sort this out. Pick up the call." Commanding. Certain.

I exhaled sharply, wiping my tears, forcing myself to breathe. My hands still shook when I picked up his call. It was a video call. I hadn't expected that. My face was raw with emotion, my lips pressed tightly together, my eyes unable to meet his.

"Yash—" I started, but my voice betrayed me.

His eyes softened immediately, but his next words made my breath hitch. "Can't I joke? Can't you take this as fun?"

I froze. For a second, I just stared at him. I had been breaking apart in that washroom, and he—he had been playing? I wanted to be mad. I wanted to throw the phone away, to yell, to demand why he would do this to me.

But I couldn't. Because beneath the anger, beneath the hurt, was something far more terrifying.

The realization. The realization that my world would stop if he wasn't in it. That no matter how much I had told myself we were just flowing with time, without labels, without expectations—I was his.

And the thought of him being someone else's? Unbearable.

"We'll talk later," I managed, cutting the call before my voice could betray me again.

Seconds later, a message popped up. "I will never leave you for another woman."

Another text. "You've set the standard too high. No one will ever match up." And then— "If we ever drift apart, it'll be because of us. Not because of someone else."

I exhaled, letting the words settle over me, easing the storm inside me just a little. Relief flooded my chest.

But then, another realization struck. How was this even possible? How had I become someone whose happiness, whose peace, whose sanity depended on a man? Hadn't I spent a lifetime guarding myself from this very thing? Hadn't I built walls thick enough to keep out exactly this kind of pain?

As I stood there with my heart still racing and his words still echoing in my mind— I knew practicality was the last thing I was capable of.

I closed my eyes, inhaling deeply, whispering a silent plea into the universe. "God, I just love this man. Keep him safe. Keep us safe."

THE RECKLESS FIRE WE COULDN'T CONTAIN

It started as a thought. A fleeting, reckless thought that should have disappeared as quickly as it came. But it didn't. It lingered. It grew. It shaped itself into something vivid, something so real that, for a moment, I let myself believe it could happen.

A weekend. Just us. Away from everything—away from responsibilities, away from the questions we refused to ask, away from the unspoken boundaries that tethered us to our separate lives. I imagined it clearly, the way fantasies sometimes unfold with too much clarity, too much precision, as if the universe is tempting you with something it knows you can never have.

I saw us driving out of the city before sunrise. The roads stretching ahead, empty and endless, the sky just beginning to lighten with soft shades of pink and orange. The hum of the car, the rhythmic sound of tires against the road, the world still asleep while we ran away from it—just for a little while.

I imagined his hand resting on my thigh, fingers tracing absentminded patterns against my jeans, his seat pushed back just enough to melt into the moment. He wasn't driving—I was. And he loved that. Said it felt good not to be the one behind the wheel for once. In real life, it was always him—long drives, no breaks, the world blurring past the windshield. But now, he just relaxed. Let go.

He'd tilt his head toward the window, eyes half-closed, soaking in the passing sky, the trees, the stillness in motion. Every now and then, he'd glance over at me with that half-smirk of his—lazy, content.

"Where to?" he'd ask, voice low.

And I'd shrug, pretending like I hadn't already traced every mile in my head a hundred times.

"Somewhere far," I'd say, letting the words breathe—letting myself breathe. "Where no one knows us."

He'd laugh—deep and soft, like velvet. The sound curled inside me, something I'd hold on to long after.

"That's the plan, then," he'd say.

And just like that, we'd be gone.

I pictured the hotel—not too polished, not too run-down. Just enough comfort to forget the world. A quiet place tucked away, maybe by the mountains, maybe near the sea. Big windows, golden afternoon light spilling in, a bed with sheets we'd tangle in, and silence. The kind that feels like peace. The kind that lets you listen to the sound of your own breathing.

Or his.

I could almost feel the crispness of the white linen against my skin, the way his warmth would seep into me as he pulled me against him. His voice—husky, lazy from the afternoon—murmuring something against my shoulder that I wouldn't quite catch, but wouldn't need to. The weight of him, the scent of him, the slow, unhurried way our bodies would fit together, like we had all the time in the world.

Except we wouldn't. We never did.

We woke up sometime in the late afternoon, the kind of waking where time doesn't feel real—just a stretch of warmth and skin and sunlight spilling through the curtains. He blinked sleep from his eyes, pulled me closer for a minute before letting out a long sigh, like even getting up felt too far away.

Eventually, we moved. Showered. Laughed about how lazy we were. Then, hungry and still wrapped in the softness of each other, we ordered lunch—his favorite: chicken lollipop, spicy and sticky; some fried rice; and chocolate-flavored milk, of course. He was almost childlike with it, grinning as he opened the carton like it was the best part of the meal.

We sat on the floor and ate straight from the boxes, music playing low again, something with a beat that made us nod along between bites. It wasn't fancy. It didn't need to be. It was good—messy, delicious, ours.

After lunch, we curled back onto the couch and picked a movie—something ridiculous, something loud.

We laughed through half of it, made dumb commentary over the other half. He rested his head in my lap, and I played with his hair, fingers tracing slow patterns across his scalp until his laughter softened into yawns.

In my mind, we'd spend the evening walking along the shore, our fingers brushing but never fully intertwining—because even in my fantasies, reality had its limits. We'd talk about nothing and everything, about our favorite songs, our childhood stories, our worst fears, our biggest dreams.

He'd stop suddenly, turn to me, and say, "If things were different, would you—?" But he wouldn't finish the question. And I wouldn't ask him to. Because the answer didn't matter. Because things weren't different.

Because this weekend only existed in the spaces between my longing and my reality. Later, in the dim glow of a hotel lamp, I'd sit on the edge of the bed, watching him from across the room.

He was standing near the huge glass window, the city lights spilling in—faint and golden across his bare shoulders. The music played low behind us, a deep, steady rhythm that felt like breath.

I walked up behind him and wrapped my arms around his waist. My cheek pressed between his shoulder blades, skin warm against skin. He was shirtless, and I could feel the quiet heat of him, the slow rise and fall of his chest. He didn't move at first, just let me hold him like that, my arms curled around him, as if I could keep the whole moment still.

"I like this," I whispered. My voice didn't echo in the room, it didn't need to. It sank into his skin like the warmth of my breath.

His hand reached down and found mine at his stomach, laced our fingers together.

Then he turned.

He looked at me like I was the only thing he saw, even with a whole city stretched out behind him. And when he kissed me, it was soft. Like remembering. Like promise.

We didn't say anything more. Just moved together, slowly, into the rhythm that had already started long before the music.

He turned to me, eyes dark with something I couldn't name—but felt. Deep. Pulling. Like gravity.

And then he pushed me gently to the bed, not rough, just sure. Like he knew exactly where I belonged in that moment.

His eyes never left mine. There was something in the way he looked at me—like I was both the question and the answer. Like he could unravel me just by touching my skin, and maybe he already had. He moved over me slow, deliberate, every breath between us thick with meaning and heat.

It was love-making, yes—if love could be a kind of poison. Sweet, slow, and sinking into every vein. I felt him everywhere, even in the places he hadn't touched yet.

Too good to be real.

Too soft to survive the morning.

But there we were—moving in time with the music we'd forgotten was still playing.

And when we broke apart, when we lay still—he reached for me again. As if letting go, even for a moment, wasn't an option.

Later, I lay on my side, eyes tracing the shape of him in the dim light—the slow rise of his chest, the curve of his back, the way his hand still found mine without thinking. He had drifted to sleep, lips parted slightly, brow smooth like he'd let something go.

But I couldn't sleep.

Not yet.

My body hummed with the after of him. The weight of his breath still lingered on my skin, the ghost of his fingers trailing across my ribs, my thighs, my spine. Everything was quiet now, but inside—somewhere soft and unguarded—I was wide awake.

It had been too much.

Too gentle.

Too real.

And yet—so painfully, impossibly good.

I turned toward him, brushing a strand of hair from his forehead, barely touching. My chest ached in that sweet, secret way—like something had cracked open, just a little.

Maybe I wasn't ready for love.

But this?

This was something else.

This was surrender.

So I closed my eyes and let myself drift too—into the warmth of him, into the silence that didn't need words, into a sleep that felt like being held.

I pictured the morning after. Waking up tangled in sheets that smelled like him. Sunlight slipping through sheer curtains, casting soft shadows on his bare back. My fingers tracing the line of his spine, memorizing the ridges of him, as if my touch alone could carve this moment into permanence.

I'd watch him stir, his eyes fluttering open, his lips curving into that slow, sleepy smile that always managed to undo me. "Morning," he'd say, voice rough with sleep. "Morning," I'd echo, my heart aching at the inevitability of the day ahead.

Because we both knew what came next. The drive back. The slow return to reality. The careful distance that would settle between us again, as if this—whatever this was—had never happened.

And maybe, as we neared the city, he'd reach for my hand, squeeze it once before letting go. A silent promise. A quiet goodbye. A reminder that, even if the world never knew about us, even if we never had more than fleeting stolen moments, this would always exist.

Here. Between us. Even if only in memory.

And then, just as suddenly as it began, the illusion shattered. Reality crashed in—sharp, cold, unforgiving.

I wasn't on a road trip with him.

I wasn't waking up beside him.

I wasn't somewhere far, where no one knew us.

I was sitting alone in my room. Phone in hand, staring at a blank screen, wondering if he was thinking about me too.

Maybe he was. Maybe he wasn't.

Maybe, in some parallel version of our lives, we had actually gone on that trip.

Maybe, in another reality, we didn't have to hide.

Maybe, in another time, in another world, we could have been more than this.

But here, in this one? We were just a story unfinished. A love never given the space to become. A weekend that never was.

There are some things in life you don't think twice about. Some people you don't hesitate for. And for me, Yash was one of them.

One evening, during one of our usual calls, I could hear the frustration in his voice. He wasn't saying it outright, but I knew—he was exhausted. Tired of being stuck in his hometown, tired of the same four walls, tired of waiting for his back to heal so he could return to Bangalore.

He missed his city. He missed the madness, the chaos, the simple routine of life that had once felt mundane but now felt like a luxury. He missed the long drives, the workdays that stretched into late nights, the sound of his car's engine roaring down the empty roads of Bangalore. And somewhere in between all of that—maybe 'he missed me.

"I just want to come back," he muttered, more to himself than to me. "I don't care about anything else. Just want to be back." There was something about the way he said it—raw, unfiltered, unguarded. It wasn't just about work. It wasn't just about the city. It was about us.

And before I could even process it, before I could think of logistics or plans or common sense, the words tumbled out of me. "I'll come and pick you up."

There was a pause. Then, a low chuckle. "You're crazy."

I wasn't joking. "I mean it. I'll drive to your place and bring you back."

He exhaled, shaking his head, amused but not surprised. He had always known this about me—I didn't shy away from doing things that others would overthink. Distance didn't scare me. Effort didn't exhaust me. Not when it came to him. And the best part? He never questioned it. He knew I was serious. He didn't tell me I was being dramatic. He didn't laugh it off. Because this was me. And with me, he never had to pretend. But still, he hesitated.

"I want my car in Bangalore. I'll need it when I start going to work again," he said, as if reasoning with himself. "The doctor says I can drive around the city, but long-distance travel is still a no."

"Fine," I said, without skipping a beat. "I'll take a flight or a bus to your place and drive back with you."

The silence stretched a little longer this time. And then, softly, "You really would, wouldn't you?"

I didn't answer. I didn't need to. Of course, I would.

For the first time in my life, distance felt like nothing. Time, responsibilities, the unspoken rules we had both learned to live by—none of it mattered in that moment. I just wanted to be with him.

I would have gone. I would have driven for hours if it meant seeing him, if it meant taking even the smallest part of his exhaustion away.

And he knew that. Maybe that's why he didn't dismiss it outright. Maybe that's why he let the idea linger between us for a little longer than necessary, letting himself imagine what it would be like—me showing up, him sliding into the passenger seat, knowing he could close his eyes, knowing he could trust me.

Because that's what we were. There was no hesitation. No overthinking. No playing it safe. Just knowing. Just being.

But eventually, like all things in life, reality crept back in.

He sighed. "Let's wait. Maybe another week or two and I'll be back."

Before I could catch my breath, the moment passed. We both knew it wouldn't happen. But the fact that I had offered? The fact that he had considered it? The fact that I would have gone in a heartbeat? That was enough.

Because in a world where everything had conditions, where love came with limits, where effort was measured and weighed before being given—we existed outside of it.

I never got in the car that day. I never made that trip. He never let me.

But that didn't change the fact that I would have. And somehow, I think that meant more than the journey itself.

The conversation was starting to fray around the edges—too many silences, too many things left unsaid. The kind of tension that builds when you're both trying too hard to be fine.

We were saying all the right things, but the warmth was slipping.

So I changed the subject. Gently.

"Can you sing for me?" I asked, trying to soften the air between us.

There was a pause on the other end. I could picture his half-smile, the way he always gets shy when I bring up his singing.

"Right now?" he asked.

I laughed lightly, trying not to sound like I needed it too much. "No... I mean, I just wish I could hear your voice even when you're far away. It gives me that... warm feeling. Like you're right here. Like the distance doesn't matter."

He was quiet for a beat. Then he said, "Okay. I'll record something for you. One song. Once I'm back. I promise."

I wanted to believe him. I did.

And for a while, that promise was enough to quiet the ache.

Three months.

That's how long it had been since I last felt the press of his body against mine, the way his breath lingered in the spaces between words, the way his touch ignited something deep within me.

Three months of pretending I wasn't waiting. But I was. Through late-night video calls, through messages that carried more weight than either of us admitted, through reels sent in the middle of a workday—silent proof that he was thinking of me.

And then, one evening, just as I was walking out of my office, my phone buzzed.

Yash- "I'm back."

Two simple words. Yet they tore something open inside me with terrifying ease.

I stared at the screen longer than necessary before my fingers typed back the only thing I could manage. "Welcome back."

We met few days later. There was no long discussion, no hesitation, no build-up. It was unspoken. It was inevitable. We always found our way back.

I had convinced myself I wouldn't overthink it. Wouldn't let anticipation crawl under my skin, wouldn't let my mind spiral into questions I wasn't ready to answer. But the second I saw him— It was over.

He stood there, framed by the doorway, like something out of a half-remembered dream. His hair— those dark, unruly curls—had grown wilder since the last time I saw him, tumbling over his forehead in a way that made me want to reach out and push them back. They suited him. Untamed, with just enough chaos to make him irresistible. Like he didn't care, and yet somehow he wore it like a man who'd walked out of a photograph that had always belonged to me.

And his scent… God, his scent. It hit me before he even moved—warm, clean, something faintly smoky, like cedar and skin warmed by sun. Familiar, but sharper now. Like he'd stepped out of the past and brought all that longing with him. I breathed it in without meaning to, and it rushed through me like something illicit.

He'd lost weight. I noticed it immediately—the sharpness in his jaw, the angles of his cheekbones more defined than before. His body had always been strong, but now it was leaner, tighter, like he had been stripped down to nothing unnecessary. And somehow, that made him even more devastating. Every inch of him looked toned, carved by time and maybe by want. He wasn't just beautiful. He was breathtaking. The kind of handsome that knocked the air out of your lungs and left you raw.

But it was his eyes that undid me. Dark, burning with something I recognized all too well. Thirst. Not just desire, but hunger. As if I was water in the desert and he hadn't had a drop in months. His gaze dragged over me, slow and deliberate, lingering a second too long at the places that made my pulse trip over itself. He was looking at me like he was starving—and I was the feast.

There was a pull between us, something electric and dangerous, snapping tight as he took a single step closer. His body gravitated toward mine instinctively, like gravity wasn't a choice anymore, just something we both had to surrender to. And when he spoke, when he exhaled my name, it wasn't just a word—it was a confession. Low and rough, like he had been holding it in his chest for months, maybe longer. Like saying it now was both a relief and a risk.

I only saw him. I couldn't see anything else. And God—he was still him. But there was something different now. Maybe it was the weight of everything unspoken hanging between us. Maybe it was the way he looked at me like I was something he lost, and now he wasn't sure if he was allowed to have me back. Or maybe it was the simple truth neither of us wanted to admit.

We had both been starving. And now we were here. It was the only warning I got before he pulled me into him. The first touch after forever.

His lips found mine in a way that felt urgent, desperate—like he was trying to erase the three months between us. Like time hadn't made us strangers in our own story. I clung to him. His hands slid down my back, pressing me closer, as if there was still distance left to erase.

The way his hands roamed me, slow at first, reverent, like he was tracing a map he'd studied a thousand times but still found new places to explore. His fingers slid down my spine with maddening precision, coaxing me to arch into him, to give in to the electricity that sparked everywhere he touched. Even in the warmth of the room, his touch made me shiver, made goosebumps rise along my skin. And when I raked my nails down his back, I felt the sharp hitch of his breath, the way his body tensed under mine. I had found his breaking point—and I reveled in it.

When we finally came together, it wasn't hurried or careless. It was deliberate. It was slow, intoxicating at first, as though we were savoring a taste we thought we'd never have again. But soon, it became something frantic, desperate, as if we both realized we had no time for slow realizations, no patience left for restraint. We clung to each other like people who understood how fragile this was, how easily it could be lost.

Because it wasn't just physical. It never had been. There was something deeper here, something neither of us dared to name out loud. But we felt it. In every stolen glance, in every ragged breath, in every time his forehead pressed against mine as we tried to catch what was left of ourselves. And for those moments, however fleeting, we weren't just bodies seeking relief. We were something more.

We kissed as if we had never been apart. And for a while, that was enough. We fell back into our rhythm. The late-night drives, the familiar, comfortable conversations, the silences that never felt empty. But more than anything— We found each other again.

Whenever we met, we were reckless. Like two people who didn't know how to slow down, how to pace ourselves. Some days, we spent hours tangled in each other's arms.

Some days, it was just thirty stolen minutes in a parked car, hands roaming, breath mingling, his fingers tracing circles on my thigh like he had no intention of stopping.

But no matter how long we had—whether it was hours or mere minutes—every moment with him felt like an ache we were only just beginning to soothe. A hunger we could barely restrain, though we tried. There was always that tension between us, a pull that neither of us could ignore, as if the universe itself conspired to bring us back together just to watch us unravel.

His lips would find the hollow of my neck, slow and deliberate, as though tasting something he'd been deprived of for too long. His mouth was warm, his breath hot against my skin, each kiss sending a shiver through me that I couldn't suppress. He wasn't rushing, but he wasn't gentle either. He kissed like a man who knew exactly how far he could push before I'd lose all control. Teasing me. Testing me.

"Do you know how much I missed this?" I whispered against his throat, my lips brushing the skin there, catching his pulse as it quickened. My voice was low, almost dangerous, the kind of tone that was equal parts promise and warning. And I knew, without him saying a word, that he had missed us too—missed this dance we did between want and need. Because every time we met— We made up for every second lost. But it wasn't just passion. It was the quiet moments in between. The moments between the fire.

The mornings when I would make toasted bread for him, watching as he bit into it with that small, satisfied hum. The way he devoured the chicken sausages I made, nodding in approval after every bite, making me feel like I had just served him a five-star meal.

The terrible tea I once made—boasting that I was great at making tea—only for him to take one sip and raise an eyebrow. "This is what you call tea?" he had smirked, setting the cup down like it had personally offended him.

"It's not that bad," I had defended, crossing my arms.

"You know what? Next time, I'm making tea for you. Then you'll know what tea is supposed to taste like."

And I had laughed, shaking my head, knowing that he would actually do it.

It was these moments that made my heart ache the most. Because no one had ever cared for me like this before. Not in the simple, unspoken ways that Yash did. He made me feel like a queen—without saying it, without trying.

And maybe that's why I fell harder every time.

THE UNSPOKEN BOUNDARIES

Fights weren't new between us. But this one was different. This wasn't the kind of argument that ended in a few hours with a "Fine, let's forget it." This wasn't about something small. This wasn't something we could laugh off later.

This one cut deep. And the worst part? I didn't see it coming. It started with my ego.

I never listened to him. I had too much pride. I held onto my independence so fiercely that sometimes, I pushed away the very people who tried to stand by me.

Yash never asked me for much. No rules. No restrictions.

Just one thing. "If you're meeting Urmi, just let me know beforehand."

That was all. Not because he doubted me, not because he wanted control, but simply because he wanted to be included in my world.

And yet, I didn't tell him this time. Not intentionally. Not because I was hiding it.

But because I didn't like the idea of being answerable to anyone.

I had spent my life making my own choices. Why should I report to anyone now? I thought it wouldn't matter. I thought he wouldn't even notice. I thought I'd tell him later, casually, in passing.

But he found out from my Instagram story. My phone vibrated the moment I posted it.

Yash: Really? You didn't think you should tell me?

I frowned at the screen. Was he serious?

Me: It was last-minute. Why are you acting like this?

And that's when he called. His voice was calm. Too calm. Controlled in a way that felt almost dangerous. "It's not about you meeting her."

"Then what is it?" I snapped.

Silence.

And then, in the quietest, most cutting way possible— "It's about the fact that you don't think I matter enough to tell me."

I felt that in my bones.

The fight escalated fast.

Me: "Why are you making this such a big deal?"

Yash: "Because I uhhh… forget it!! You won't understand.

That was the moment. The moment his voice cracked. The moment I realized this wasn't about the meeting. This wasn't about Urmi.

This was about me. About how I always shut him out. About how I made him feel like he wasn't important enough. About how, deep down, he knew I was still fighting this. Fighting us.

And then, he said something that broke me. "You just don't believe in love, do you?" I should have expected this from you. A cold, brutal statement. Not an accusation. A fact.

And the worst part? He was right.

Morning arrived, but I barely felt it. Sleep had been restless, my mind replaying our argument, my stubbornness, his frustration. The silence between us stretched longer than I could handle.

Twelve hours. That's how long it took me to finally admit what I had been refusing to see. I needed him. Not just his messages. Not just his voice. Not just the way he made me feel when we were together. I needed the way he cared, the way he fought for me, the way he wanted me to understand him—not for his sake, but for ours.

And when that realization hit me, I texted him. "Can we talk?"

The three dots appeared immediately, disappearing just as fast. Then, his response—cold, clipped.

"For what? If you're not willing to listen or understand me?"

A lump formed in my throat. I hated this. I hated knowing that I had hurt him, that I had pushed him away when all he wanted was something as simple as a heads-up about where I was.

But still—my ego. My pride. My stubbornness. We texted back and forth, short, tense responses. He was exhausted. Done. And when I finally gathered the courage to say something more, my phone rang. He was calling me.

For a second, I considered not picking up. Not because I didn't want to talk, but because I wasn't ready to back down.

But I answered.

"What do you want me to say?" he asked, his voice calm but distant. "You never listen, so what's the point?"

I swallowed, gripping my phone tighter. "I do listen."

"No, you don't." His sigh was heavy, tired. "I'm just upset because you don't understand me. Or worse—you don't even try to."

I felt a sharp pang of guilt. Because he was right. He never asked me to change. Never told me what to do, who to meet, where to go. He only wanted to know. To be aware. To feel included in the life he had made space for me in.

But I had made everything so difficult. For what? For ego? For control? For my inability to accept that sometimes, love doesn't have to be complicated?

He had always been clear about his feelings. About me. About us.

And maybe—maybe I was the one complicating things.

I exhaled, closing my eyes. "I'm sorry."

There was a pause. A beat of silence that stretched too long.

And then, his voice—softer this time. "Why do you make it so hard to love you?"

Something inside me cracked. I pressed my fingers against my temple, my chest tightening. "I don't know."

But I did. Because I didn't trust love. Because I had never been loved the way he loved me. Because I was scared of what would happen if I let myself believe in it.

And yet, here he was. Still here. Still choosing me.

The silence between us shifted—less tense, less heavy.

"I'll see you soon?" he asked, as if he already knew the answer.

"Yeah," I whispered.

Because I wasn't ready to lose him.

We were both busy—always busy. Caught up in our lives, tangled in deadlines and obligations and the thousand things that make up adulthood. Work pulled us in opposite directions. Personal commitments ate up whatever time we had left. We were at different stages of life, running on parallel tracks that never seemed to line up, no matter how much we wanted them to.

And we did want them to. We wanted to be there for each other, to find time, to hold space. But wanting wasn't always enough. Sometimes I failed him—forgot to call back, cancelled last minute, let exhaustion win. And sometimes he failed me—got caught up in work, promised to text and didn't, disappeared into his own world for days. Neither of us meant to. But that's how it goes sometimes, doesn't it? That's how things start to fray. Slowly. Quietly.

At first, it was subtle. The little things you brush off because they seem harmless. A message seen but left unanswered until later—until later became too late. Calls that went straight to voicemail because it wasn't a good time, plans that once felt smooth and uncomplicated, that once needed nothing more than a glance and a grin, now felt like a logistical nightmare. Rescheduling. Rearranging. Sacrificing. We still made the effort... until we didn't. Or until we did, but it didn't feel the same.

The intensity between us? That never faded. But the urgency... that did. The need to see each other, to hear each other, to hold each other close—it was still there, but muted. Dull around the edges. And that was when the fights crept back in. They weren't explosive. They weren't even about big things. It was the small things that started to sting. The quiet disappointments. The unanswered needs.

We never fought about love. Never about loyalty or trust. It was always about the cracks that had been there from the start—the ones we'd once been too wrapped up in each other to notice. A text that I didn't answer soon enough. A call he made when I was already half-asleep, too tired to talk. A date we planned and postponed, then cancelled because life got in the way again.

And I could feel it. We were slipping. Not because we didn't care. But because life didn't leave us enough space to show it. We weren't getting the time to remind ourselves why this mattered. Why we mattered.

I wanted to fix it. God, I wanted to fix it. I wanted to see him more. To be near him. To grab onto the pieces of us that still felt solid. But every time I brought it up, every time I tried to say the things I was feeling, the conversation cracked apart. It turned into frustration. He would sigh, rub his face, and say, "I'm doing my best."

And I believed him. I did. But sometimes your best isn't enough. I wanted to say that. "I know. But it's not enough." I wanted to say it, but I didn't. Because I knew how much that would hurt. I knew that pushing harder might break something we were barely holding together as it was.

And yet, as the weeks passed, I couldn't ignore it. The space between us wasn't measured in miles or hours anymore. It was in silence. In the way we stopped telling each other the small things. In the way we filled in the gaps with assumptions instead of words. Emotional distance. The kind that feels impossible to bridge.

I knew he still cared. I never doubted that. But I started wondering if caring was enough. Was it enough to sustain something that had always lived on intensity? On stolen moments and urgent need? We weren't those people anymore. We didn't have the luxury of time, or the recklessness we once did. And I wasn't sure we knew how to love each other from a distance.

One evening, after another cancelled plan, another postponed dinner, another message that ended with both of us too tired to argue, I found myself staring at my phone. Just staring. Waiting for his name to flash on the screen. Waiting for the sound of his voice saying my name like it still meant something.

And for the first time, I wondered—had we already lost this? Or were we just too exhausted to keep holding on?

The night before I left for Pune, Yash was restless. I could hear it in the way he breathed on the other end of the line—slow, steady, too deliberate. Like he was trying to convince himself he was fine. Like if he kept his voice level enough, he might even believe it.

"You're all packed?" he asked, casual. Too casual. His tone was like a coat thrown carelessly over a chair, but I could hear the edge beneath it. Sharp and uncomfortable.

"Almost," I murmured, stretching out across my bed. The fan hummed overhead, and the sheets were cool against my skin, but the heat in his question clung to me. My phone was pressed to my ear, and for a moment,

I closed my eyes, trying to pretend this was just another call. But it wasn't.

There was a pause. That kind of pause where you know what's coming before they say it, and you still brace yourself anyway.

"Your boss will be there, right?" he asked, and this time, there was no pretending. He wasn't asking because he didn't know. He already knew. He just needed to hear me say it.

I exhaled slowly. There it was—the thing neither of us had wanted to touch all evening. The undercurrent. The thing we'd danced around through half-hearted jokes and stretched silences.

"Yes," I said. Honest. Always honest with him. That had been our thing from the beginning. No games. No lies. Just truth, even when it was hard.

And it was hard. Because Yash didn't like my boss. Not because he was my superior, or because we spent long hours on projects together, but because once—months ago, in passing, in a moment that didn't even seem to matter—my boss had admitted he liked me. Liked me more than he should. And I had told Yash. Because I tell Yash everything.

I told him how I shut it down immediately. How it wasn't serious. How I'd made sure there was no room for misunderstanding. But logic doesn't always quiet the parts of us that feel too much. And Yash felt too much when it came to me. He always had.

"Hm," he said, but it wasn't just a sound. It was the scrape of teeth against his bottom lip. The twitch in his jaw when he was holding something back. I could picture him so clearly—leaning against his balcony railing, running his hand through his curls like he did when he was trying to keep himself grounded. His fingers threading through them, then tugging, sharp. His eyes dark, distant, but burning.

"Yash," I said softly. "Nothing's going to happen."

"I know." But his voice was too flat. Too resigned. It wasn't conviction; it was him trying to convince himself that knowing me was the same as knowing the world around me. And it wasn't. Not for him.

The silence stretched, long and heavy. I could feel it settling on my chest, warm and uncomfortable. I could feel him thinking. And that was almost worse than hearing him say it.

"Do you trust me?" I asked, and my voice cracked a little on the words, even though I tried to keep it steady.

"It's not about that," he said, quick. Too quick.

It never was. Yash trusted me. I never doubted that. What he didn't trust was the world. He didn't trust circumstance, or chance, or people who said things they shouldn't when I was too polite to walk away fast enough. It wasn't about me. It was about everything he couldn't control.

"I just don't like it," he admitted finally. His voice had softened, but there was steel underneath it. "Him being around you. Talking to you. I don't like the way he looks at you."

I let out a slow breath. I understood. God, I did. I wasn't used to this—someone caring enough to be afraid of losing me. No one had ever worried about where I was or who I was with. No one had cared enough to mind. And here he was. Caring. Worrying. Fighting with himself. Fighting with me, too, because he didn't know where else to put it.

And I liked it. That was the truth I couldn't tell him. I liked that he cared. That I mattered enough to make him restless. That his jealousy wasn't a wound, but a mark of how tightly he held me.

"I'll call you before I sleep," I said, and it was more than a promise. It was an offering.

"Yeah," he muttered. "You better."

But there was a warmth in it. That rough edge of his affection, threaded through every word, every unspoken plea. Stay mine. That's what he was really saying.

I smiled to myself as I lay there, listening to the quiet on the other end of the line. Even though I was leaving in the morning, even though I was heading to a different city, a different life for a few days, it felt like I was carrying him with me.

Maybe that was the thing about us. No matter where we went, no matter how far, we were always tethered. Even when it hurt.

A STORM NAMED DISTANCE

Pune was cold when I landed. Not gentle, not refreshing—sharp. A cold that crept into your bones and stayed there. I welcomed it, in a way. The chill dulled everything else. My exhaustion. My mind. The ache of being stretched thin by work, by people demanding more than I had to give.

I told myself I was fine with the distance. With the time apart. That I needed this space, these days away from him.

But Yash… Yash was never good at distance. The messages started as polite check-ins.

Hope you reached safe. Busy?

And yes, I was busy. Buried under meetings I didn't want to be in, dinners I didn't want to sit through. I was running on autopilot, smiling when I had to, saying the right things, while my brain screamed for quiet. By the time I finally shut the hotel room door behind me at night, I was too spent to be anything but silent.

But silence only makes some men restless.

By the time I noticed his name on my screen again, there was a missed call.

And then, at 1:07 a.m.:

Where are you?

I frowned. In my room. Why? I shot back, sharper than I meant to.

His reply was instant. Are you alone?

I exhaled, long and slow, rubbing my temples like it could massage away the heat rising in me. Of course I'm alone. Who else would be here?

The dots flickered. Then vanished. Then his words: I don't know. That's why I asked.

There it was—the thing he held back all day, the thing he only let out at night when it was quiet and he was too tired to lie to himself. His mind playing tricks. His gut twisting at the thought of me somewhere he couldn't reach.

I wanted to be angry. I wanted to tell him to stop. But I didn't. Because I could feel him unraveling. And that did something to me. He wasn't accusing me. He wasn't doubting me. He just hated that I wasn't there. And maybe, I hated it too. I just didn't know how to say it.

Yash, I typed. I don't like this.

It took him longer this time. I don't like it either. But I can't stand knowing you're there and I can't do anything about it.

Another pause. I can't stand the thought of you around him.

I closed my eyes. I told you—he means nothing to me.

I know. It's not about him. It's about me. About the fact you're not here. You're not in Bangalore. You're not...

Another pause. With me.

That hit something raw inside me. Because no one had ever said that to me before. Not like that. Not so openly. So broken. So real. And it kept coming.

Come back, he sent. Just... come back soon.

I don't care if you're tired. I'll pick you up from the airport. I'll re-schedule your tickets if I have to. I just want you back here.

I stared at the screen, my body tensed between exhaustion and anger, irritation and something dangerously close to need. I'm working, Yash. I'm here for work. I hated how defensive I sounded.

I know, he replied. But that doesn't stop me from wanting you. And then, I need you here.

I sat there for a while, glaring at my phone like it was his fault. Like he was the one pulling me in two directions. But it wasn't his fault. It was mine. For pretending I didn't want that. For pretending his possessiveness didn't make me feel wanted in ways I'd never been. For acting like his restlessness was a burden, when it was the first time anyone had ever found it hard to let me go.

I sighed. My anger cooled into something heavier, but warmer.

He was messy. He was possessive. But he was mine. And God, how I had wanted to be someone's. Wanted to be missed like this. Wanted to be the thing someone couldn't stand to be far from.

I typed slowly. I'm coming back soon. And when I do… you better be ready to deal with me.

His reply came fast. I've been ready.

And I smiled. Finally.

Because no matter how far I went, how hard I fought to stay detached, I knew this: I'd always come back to him. And he would always be waiting.

Coming back from Pune, I was restless in a way I couldn't explain. My body was back in Bangalore, but my mind was stuck on one loop: I need to see him. It had been days since I last saw Yash, but they felt longer than they should have. Like time was stretching itself thin just to test me. I caught myself replaying moments in my head—his voice, the way his hand brushed against mine without thinking, how his eyes softened in that way they only did when it was just us.

I was counting down minutes that weren't even promised yet. Making mental notes—when we could meet, where, what I'd say when I saw him, how I'd make fun of his ridiculous possessiveness before giving in to it completely.

But life… life didn't care.

We couldn't meet. No matter how much we wanted to, no matter how much we promised ourselves we'd make it happen. Life had a way of interfering—small things, ordinary things, but they piled up like bricks between us.

And yet, we spoke. Occasionally, when we could carve out a few minutes between the chaos. And we texted. Almost every day. Little messages that filled the spaces where we couldn't be. Sometimes it was something as simple as, Did you eat? Or, How was your meeting? Other times, it was just a photo of something random.

It wasn't one big thing that kept us apart. It was small things.

His family needing him. My deadlines closing in. His late meetings. My early mornings. And somewhere in between, we kept trying to carve out a sliver of time for just us.

"Tomorrow?" I'd ask, hopeful.

"Can't. Work dinner," he'd reply, tired. "What about the weekend?"

"Saturday is packed with family stuff. Sunday?"

"Maybe Sunday evening. I'll let you know."

Always maybe. Always I'll let you know.

We made plans. And then we cancelled them. We promised next time. And then next time came and went. Days passed. Then a week. Then two.

Two whole weeks after I got back before we finally saw each other again.

And in between? The texts, the calls, the silences. The tiny, constant ache of wanting more and settling for less because there wasn't another option. But even through the frustration, I knew this: He was there. He was trying. And so was I.

And sometimes, when his name flashed on my screen at midnight with nothing but *"Miss you"*, it was enough.

Not quite the same as hearing it whispered against my skin, but enough to keep me holding on until it was real again.

But when we did— It was like no time had passed at all.

The moment I saw him, it was as if my body recognized something before my mind could catch up. Like my skin had been holding onto the memory of him, waiting for the moment he'd be close again. I wasn't prepared for the intensity of it.

For the way my heartbeat quickened when I spotted him standing there, waiting for me. The way his face broke into a soft, knowing smile, like he already understood everything I was feeling without me having to say a word.

There were no grand gestures, no elaborate words. Just a quiet moment of us—slipping into something that had been missing, something that felt like home.

When he pulled me into his arms, I melted. Because this—this was what I had been waiting for. All the waiting, all the distance, all the restless nights wondering when we'd finally have a moment to just be—it all disappeared in that instant.

His scent, his warmth, the way his arms wrapped around me, firm yet unhurried. The way he held me as if grounding himself, as if this was as much a relief for him as it was for me. He pressed his forehead against mine, exhaling slowly.

"You have no idea how much I missed you."

And in that moment, I knew— No matter how long we had to wait, no matter how many times life kept us apart, we would always find our way back to this.

Because this was us. A cycle of distance and reunion. A pattern of longing and fulfillment. A rhythm we had learned to live with.

It had been a long day for him. I could see it the moment he walked in—the slump of his shoulders, the tired drag of his steps, the way he exhaled slowly, rubbing the back of his neck. He didn't have to say anything. His exhaustion spoke for him.

"Rough day?" I asked, watching as he sank onto the couch, his head tilting back against the cushions.

"The worst," he murmured, closing his eyes.

I hesitated for a moment before walking over to him, standing just behind the couch. Slowly, I placed my hands on his shoulders, feeling the tension knotted beneath my fingertips. His muscles were tight, coiled with the weight of the day.

"Want a massage?" I asked.

His head tilted slightly, opening one eye to look at me, curiosity flickering through his exhaustion. "You give massages?"

"I have never given a massage to anyone, but I can try," I said, standing behind him, my fingers hesitating just above his shoulders.

He let out a low chuckle, tilting his head slightly to look at me. "You sure? You don't have to."

"You look like you need it," I shrugged, forcing a casual tone even though something about this felt... different. "So just sit still and let me try."

He leaned forward slightly, exposing the broad expanse of his back to me, and for a brief moment, I hesitated. I had never done this before. Never touched anyone like this. But with him? It didn't feel unnatural. It felt... right.

I placed my hands on his shoulders, feeling the warmth of his skin beneath the fabric of his t-shirt. His muscles were tense—tight knots of stress buried beneath the weight of work, responsibilities, and whatever else he never spoke about. I pressed down gently, unsure of how much pressure to apply, testing.

"Mmm," he hummed, shifting slightly beneath my hands. "Not bad."

I laughed softly, rolling my thumbs over the knots in his shoulders. "Not bad? I just started."

"Exactly," he murmured, exhaling as I moved lower, working into the tension along his spine. "If this is you trying, I can't wait for you to get better at it." His words sent a flicker of warmth through me, but I pushed it aside, focusing on my movements. Slow. Deep. Trying to feel where he needed it most.

At first, I was nervous—worried I'd press too hard, that I'd get it wrong. But as I found my rhythm, as I felt his body ease under my touch, I realized something. I liked this. Not just because I was helping him relax, but because for the first time, I was the one taking care of him.

He was always the one making sure I was okay, always the one holding me, shielding me, feeding me the first bite of his food like it was second nature. But now? Now, I got to take care of him.

"God," he sighed as I pressed my thumbs into a particularly tight knot, his head dropping forward. "That feels unreal."

I smiled, my fingers moving with more confidence now, kneading into the tension, feeling his body respond to my touch. I could feel the way his muscles slowly softened, the way his breath deepened, the way he was letting go in a way he rarely did.

For twenty minutes, I worked through the stress in his back, his shoulders, his neck. And for twenty minutes, he let me. When I finally pulled back, shaking my hands out, he turned to look at me, his gaze slow and heavy with something unreadable.

"I can't believe you just did that," he said, his voice thick with exhaustion but laced with something else—something softer. "That was… perfect."

I shrugged, trying to play it off even though my heart was still racing. "Told you I could try."

"Try?" He smirked, his eyes glinting with something playful. "I think you just signed yourself up for life."

In no time, it became our thing. After a long day, after hours of exhaustion weighing down on him, he would look at me with that small smirk and say—

"Massage?"

And I would always say yes. Because I loved it. I loved watching his face relax, loved the way his body melted under my touch, loved knowing that I could take away at least some of his stress.

Loved that, in my own quiet way, I could take care of him too.

We were back to our rhythm. Reels sent at odd hours. Inside jokes woven into everyday conversations. The morning texts—sometimes just a simple "Good morning, babe", sometimes longer, thoughtful, carrying the weight of things left unsaid.

It felt so good. Too good. Because I knew by now— life never let us hold onto things for too long.

THE SECRET LANGUAGE OF LOVE

It was late when Yash called. His voice was low, casual, but there was something underneath it. Restlessness maybe. Or something heavier he wasn't saying.

"What are you doing?" he asked.

"Nothing much," I replied, closing my laptop with a sigh. I was tired, but not enough to say no. Not when it was him.

"Can you step out for the night?" he asked, like it was the most natural thing in the world. Like we did this all the time.

I paused. "What's the plan?"

There was a beat of silence, and then his familiar honesty, simple and unfiltered.

"No plan. I'm starving. Let's eat first. Then… I just want to spend some time with you."

He didn't elaborate. He didn't have to. I understood what he meant. What he needed. What I needed too, even if I hadn't realized it until he said it out loud.

"I'll pick you up in an hour," he added, before I could think too hard about it.

And an hour later, he was there.

He rolled down the window when I stepped in, his arm resting casually on the door.

"Find us a place for Chinese?" he said, glancing over at me with that half-smile that always disarmed me more than I wanted to admit.

He wasn't dressed for anything formal—just joggers and a T-shirt—but he made it look good, like he always did. Relaxed, like there was nowhere else he needed to be.

I scrolled through my phone while he drove, narrowing it down to a quiet place not too far away. We didn't say much on the drive. We didn't have to. It was easy, familiar. The kind of quiet that settles between two people who already understand each other.

The restaurant was small, tucked into a quieter part of the city, still open late enough for us. We ordered quickly, and he ate like he meant it—like he'd been too busy to remember food until now.

I watched him between bites, thinking how often we forgot to just stop and be here. Just this.

Afterward, he looked at me, his expression thoughtful.

"Do you want to head back to your place?" he asked.

I shook my head. No

He nodded like he already knew that. Like he wasn't really asking.

"We could… find a place?" he said simply.

No hesitation. No assumptions. Just an offer. A suggestion that sounded less like a plan and more like a need for space. Time. Quiet.

And so we did.

We found a hotel nearby, something simple, and checked in. No fuss. No long explanations. It was easy, almost instinctive, like we both understood we didn't want the night to end yet. Like we were just looking for somewhere the world couldn't follow us.

The room was clean, quiet, the lights warm. He kicked his shoes off, stretched out for a moment on the edge of the bed like he was finally letting himself breathe.

I dropped my bag by the chair, sitting down beside him without a word.

Sometimes, it wasn't about the place. It was about finding a little time that belonged just to us. And that was enough. He closed the door behind me, his fingers lingering on the handle for a second longer before he turned to look at me.

"Come here," he said, his voice softer now. And I did.

We did what we always did—talked. About everything. About nothing. About work. About old memories. About stupid things that made us laugh until our sides hurt. A night of conversations, music, and something more.

And just as he leaned back with that boyish smile— the one he uses when he's most at ease—I tilted my head and said, "You know… this feels like the perfect time to bring something up."

He looked at me, already suspicious. "What now?"

"The song," I said, gently nudging his arm. "You promised me a recording. Remember? Back when you were pretending to be all sentimental and far away."

He laughed, caught. "You mean my chart-topping hit that exists only in theory?"

"Yes. That one. I've been waiting. Very patiently, might I add."

He pulled me closer, his lips brushing my temple. "Maybe I'm saving it for a moment like this."

"Uh-huh," I teased. "That's your excuse for everything."

He just smiled—and kissed me. The kind of kiss that didn't ask permission, didn't need to. The kind that said we already knew how this night would end.

And maybe it was the music. Or the glow of old memories. Or the fact that laughter always made us softer.

But slowly, the conversation melted into touches. Into quiet. Into something deeper.

We made love the way we always did when words ran out—with tenderness, with heat, with that knowing rhythm that comes only when you've memorized someone's breath.

It wasn't rushed. It wasn't loud.

It was everything. And then, it was still.

After, I lay there, his arm around me, the world quiet except for our breaths.

I smiled to myself, eyes closed. "Still waiting on that song, by the way."

He groaned, burying his face in my shoulder. "Woman, you're relentless."

"And you love it."

He kissed my skin like punctuation. "Yeah. I really do."

Music was always our thing. The one thing that connected us in ways words never could. There was something about sharing music with someone. The way lyrics could say what we were too afraid to. The way a melody could slip between the spaces of silence, filling it with meaning.

That night, as we lay back, his playlist played softly in the background, a mix of old favorites and new discoveries. I closed my eyes, letting it wash over me, letting the night pull me into something deeper.

And then— "Close your eyes," he whispered.

I turned to him. "What?"

He smiled, but it wasn't his usual teasing smirk. It was something softer, something almost vulnerable. "Just close your eyes," he repeated. "Hug me. Hold me tightly."

A shiver ran through me. I hesitated, but only for a second. And then, I moved closer, wrapping my arms around him, pressing myself into him, feeling his warmth seep into my skin. His arms came around me too, his grip firm yet gentle, as if he was trying to memorize the shape of me.

And then, he played the song. The song that said everything we never did. It started slow. A soft, haunting melody. And then, the words—

If I start writing, may you come to me

If I sit to write, may you sit with me,

May you rest your head on my shoulder,

If I say sleep, may you fall asleep,

Come, let me recite a poem,

And let every word I say become real,

If I write heart, may you hold yours,

If I take a breath, may you sigh,

If I write restlessness, may you feel it,

Then may I break that restlessness,

So that you find a little peace…

I felt the meaning of each word settle in my chest, pressing into me, slipping into the spaces between my ribs. I didn't move. Neither did he.

The room had disappeared. The world had disappeared. There was only this moment, only the sound of our breathing, the warmth of his skin against mine, the unspoken ache between us. I didn't know if he had chosen the song for me. Or if it had chosen us.

But in that moment, it didn't matter. Because it was saying all the things we hadn't said. Because it was saying everything.

I exhaled, my breath shaky, my fingers gripping the fabric of his t-shirt. He didn't let go. Not yet. His hand slid up my back, slow, deliberate. His fingers found my hair, tangled in it, tracing lazy circles that sent a slow fire through me.

I opened my eyes, just slightly, enough to see him watching me. His gaze was heavy. Searching. As if he was memorizing me, just as I was memorizing him.

"Yash," I whispered, not even knowing what I was trying to say. He didn't answer. He just pulled me closer. And in that moment, I knew— This wasn't just another night. This wasn't just another song. This was us. Raw. Unfiltered. Unsaid.

A love that had no definition, no promises, no guarantees. But a love that existed. Somewhere between a whispered lyric and a heartbeat. Somewhere in the way I fit perfectly into his arms. Somewhere in the way he had chosen to spend this night with me, in the way he had asked me to come, in the way he had wanted me there.

Maybe this wasn't forever. Maybe we would wake up tomorrow and pretend like none of this had ever happened.

But right now— Right now, this night belonged to us.

His touch still lingered on my skin, his voice— low and teasing—echoed in the back of my mind. The warmth of him, of us, hadn't faded yet.

But the quiet always comes.

And when it did, it carried me here.

Now, sitting on the terrace of my sister's apartment— about ten days later—that night feels both close and impossibly far. I pulled my knees to my chest, arms wrapped around them. The cold breeze tugged at the loose strands of my hair, and the city stretched out in front of me, restless but distant. I wasn't really watching it. I was somewhere else entirely.

It had been more than ten days since I last saw him. And somehow, it felt longer than it should have. I'd been surrounded by people—family, cousins, endless chatter filling the rooms—but I couldn't shake the feeling of something missing. Like an itch I couldn't quite reach. An emptiness that didn't make sense on paper, but was real all the same.

I missed him. Not just his presence. Not his hands or his mouth or even his voice. I missed the way he made time for me. The way he carved out these spaces, hidden from the world, where it was just us. I missed being someone's priority when everything else was screaming for attention.

As I sat there, letting my head fall back against the wall, the memories came uninvited, but I welcomed them.

The first one was quiet. A morning. Early.

The city was still half-asleep, and I should've been, too. But he came anyway. Before work. Before his phone started ringing and the world pulled him back in.

Even when he was late, he found a way to show up.

He'd lean against my kitchen counter, sipping water from the glass he always reached for like he lived there. Watching me toast bread and chicken sausages like we were something domestic, something simple.

He always ate the first bite while standing, his bag slung over his shoulder, keys jingling quietly in his hand.

And before he left, he always held me for just a second longer than necessary, like he was reluctant to let go. Like a man stealing warmth before stepping out into the cold.

And then, another memory followed.

One random weekend.

I was out with Urmi and a few others, laughing, pretending I wasn't counting the hours since I'd last heard from him.

And then my phone buzzed. Him. Wait near her place for a few minutes. That's all he said. No explanation. No need for one.

I waited. Parked my car in a quiet corner and tapped my fingers against the steering wheel, wondering why I was there. Wondering why I always said yes.

He arrived a few minutes later, in his own car—his family with him. But even in that crowd, even in that moment of pretending, his eyes found mine.

And then that grin. Wide. Unfiltered. Childlike.

The kind of smile that made everything else blur.

We didn't dare to cross paths. Couldn't. Shouldn't. And we didn't need to.

A buzz on my phone.

No words. Just a hug. A kiss. Two quiet emojis carrying more than any sentence ever could.

He kept grinning—like just seeing me had cracked something open inside him.

And before anyone could see too much, read too far into it, I pulled away. Drove off with my heart full and heavy all at once.

That look on his face?

It stayed. Long after.

Tucked into me like a secret I didn't know how to hold—but couldn't bear to let go of.

The third memory came rushing in just as fast.

A festival night. The air was thick with celebration. I was at a friend's place, smiling at people, having fun and dancing.

Then my phone buzzed. Where are you?

At a friend's place. Why?

Can you meet?

And I knew I shouldn't.

He was at home. With his family. With people who expected him to be fully there. But he wasn't. Because he made time. For me.

I slipped away, heart pounding, found a quiet stretch of road where we could be alone for a moment. When I saw him waiting there, hands shoved in his pockets, I felt it.

That quiet certainty. No labels. No explanations. But he was mine.

He reached for my hands as soon as I was close enough. Held them like he was anchoring both of us. His thumb ran slowly over my knuckles, back and forth, like he was memorizing something he already knew.

"You okay?" he asked softly.

I nodded. "Better now."

And that was it. No grand gestures. No fireworks. Just him showing up when it mattered.

I opened my eyes and stared up at the sky. The city noise seemed farther away now. Isn't this what love is?

The kind that doesn't need to be shouted from rooftops. The kind that exists quietly, in gestures no one else sees. In a man who makes time for you before work. Who waits until the night is quiet to steal a moment. Who asks you to wait just for a glimpse.

It wasn't loud. But it was real.

I leaned back against the terrace railing, my chest heavy, but full. I missed him. A week more before I'd see him. A week more before I'd get to hold him again.

But until then, I had this. These memories. Ours. And they were enough. For now.

THE CONVERSATION THAT CHANGED EVERYTHING

I was just back from my sister's place. As usual, we hadn't been able to meet.

We'd been texting that morning—going in circles, talking about *us*, or whatever this thing was. He said I didn't understand him. That I didn't *listen*. Maybe he was right. Maybe I was just tired. Or maybe we were both saying things without really meaning to say them.

But it was a weekday. Work loomed. And neither of us wanted to ruin the day.

So we paused. We said we'd talk in the evening. Let it breathe.

And when the call finally came, it started like it always did. That familiar moment—him, stepping out of the office, voice softer, more his, as the city melted behind him. That quiet in-between space he shared with me. Between his world and mine.

Where we weren't quite friends. Weren't quite anything else. Just… us.

Usually, there'd be something light to start with. A silly story. A joke. Teasing. The comfortable banter we slipped into without trying.

But tonight… tonight felt different.

The usual ease between us had frayed. I noticed it in the way he paused more than usual. In the way I kept waiting for him to say something he wasn't saying.

I could feel it in the way he said my name. Like it was carrying weight.

Like something had been sitting on his chest all day, waiting for a crack to spill out.

"You okay?" I asked, keeping my tone light, but already bracing myself.

There was a pause. Then, his voice—lower than usual, clipped. "You never listen."

I blinked. "Excuse me?"

"You don't listen," he said again, firmer now. "You never really hear what I'm trying to say. You just… steamroll through. Always have."

I frowned, my spine straightening. "Where is this coming from?"

He didn't raise his voice. That wasn't his style. But there was something colder in it. Controlled. Calculated.

"You have too much ego. You ruin things before they even have a chance to become anything. You say you want closeness, but the second it starts to get real—you shut down. You act like you're above it all."

"Wow," I said, the word bitter on my tongue. "That's rich, coming from you."

He didn't flinch. "And you never take responsibility. You just push things away. Brush them off. Make jokes. Change the subject. Pretend it's all nothing. But it's not nothing. It never was."

His voice had gone quieter now, but the sharpness was still there. And it cut through me in all the places I didn't want to look too closely at.

I felt the heat rise in my chest—my body preparing to defend itself. I wanted to argue. To throw his flaws back at him like darts. But I didn't. Because under the sting, I knew.

He wasn't wrong.

And it terrified me how much that realization hurt.

"I know," I said finally, my voice smaller than I intended. "I know I do that."

There was a pause. A long one. I wondered if he was surprised I'd admitted it. I was surprised myself.

"I don't mean to," I added, quieter still. "It's not that I don't care. It's just… easier. To pretend. To act like it's fine. Like I'm fine."

He didn't speak for a long while, and for a moment, I thought he'd hung up. But then—

"I don't want you to be fine," he said, and there was something softer now, something that almost broke me. "I want you to be real."

I swallowed hard. The silence between us now wasn't comfortable. It was raw. Necessary.

And in that moment, with the quiet humming through the line like a heartbeat, I realized something terrifying:

He wasn't asking me to fix it. He was asking me to show up.

There was silence on the other end of the call. A silence that asked me to continue. A silence that gave me the space to speak without judgment. I took a deep breath, gathering my thoughts.

"It's just…" I hesitated. "Where I come from, I've never really had anyone to listen. Not really. I've spent the last twenty years wanting to talk, wanting to say things, but there was nobody to listen. My family… they're just busy with their own lives, their own priorities. So I got used to keeping everything to myself."

I let out a shaky breath, my fingers gripping the edge of my bedsheet. "It's a habit now. Guarding myself. Not sharing. Not expecting anyone to care."

Another pause. And then, his voice—calmer, softer. "But I care."

Those three words felt heavier than they should have.

"I want you to share," he continued. "At least with me. If not with anyone else, then just with me."

I closed my eyes. How did he always know exactly what to say? "When you say something, I want to react," he admitted. "I want to respond, to give suggestions, to be there for you. But you don't let me."

I stayed silent.

"Let me be there," he said simply. "That's all I ask."

It was such a simple thing. Let him be there. And yet, it felt like the hardest thing in the world. But before the conversation could turn any heavier, he did what he always did. He made it lighter.

"So..." his tone shifted, teasing now. "When are we meeting?"

I let out a small laugh, grateful for the change in energy.

"A quick breakfast, maybe," I said, trying to match his tone. "Just a peaceful one hour at my place."

"How about Friday?" I suggested.

He nodded, even though I couldn't see him. "Friday, then."

"But I only have an hour," he reminded me.

I pretended to sigh. "Fine. Hmmm."

Before I could process it, the tension of the night dissolved into something else. Something simpler. Something that made my chest feel warm again. Because that's what made him special. Not grand gestures. Not over-the-top words. But the way he always made time. Even when he didn't have it. Even when life was pulling him in a million different directions. Even when the world expected him to be somewhere else. He chose to be with me. That's what made us special.

Friday came faster than I expected.

And so did he.

I didn't bother with breakfast, didn't set the table, didn't do any of the things I told myself I might.

Because when Yash texted "Five minutes away", all I felt was the familiar pull of him.

And five minutes later, there he was—at my door, with that look he always had when he saw me after a stretch of days apart.

Like relief.

Like need.

Like he was home.

I barely got out a "Hey" before he stepped inside, shutting the door behind him with a quiet finality that sent a rush through me.

Then it was him—his hands on my waist, pulling me in like he couldn't wait another second. His mouth found mine, hungry and unspoken, and I didn't hesitate. My fingers curled into the soft fabric of his hoodie, needing him closer, needing him here.

His kiss started slow—like he wanted to memorize me all over again—but it didn't stay that way. It never did.

Because with us, slow was a luxury we rarely had.

And we were already burning through the seconds.

The air around us shifted—thick with the kind of urgency that came from too many days apart and too many things left unsaid. He pressed me back against the wall, and I welcomed it, the weight of him, the warmth, the way his body folded so easily into mine.

Clothes became an afterthought. Hoodie. T-shirt. Fingers fumbling with zippers, pulling fabric aside with that familiar impatience that was somehow always tender. We moved through the room like we didn't care where we ended up, only that we got there together.

There was breathless laughter when we stumbled into the edge of the couch, a gasp when his mouth found the curve of my neck, and the kind of silence that only comes when two people are too full of each other to speak.

We made love like the world had narrowed down to skin and breath and the soft, aching rhythm of reunion.

There was nothing rushed in how we moved—but it was urgent. Like we were trying to make up for lost time, knowing we never really could.

He knew exactly where to touch, how to hold me, how to move so that my name came undone in a whisper.

And I knew him too—every sound he made, every shift in his breath, was a story I had read over and over and still couldn't get enough of.

It was messy. It was deep. It was the kind of passion built on history, on muscle memory, on the ache of wanting that never truly goes away.

And when it was over—when we finally let the stillness find us—he held me there, heart pounding against mine.

His forehead pressed against mine, both of us catching our breath, neither of us ready to let go.

"I missed you," he said, his voice low, rough at the edges like it had come from somewhere deeper.

"I know," I whispered, my hands still resting on his chest. "I missed you too."

But we didn't need to say it again.

It was already there. In every touch. In every kiss. In every desperate, beautiful second of that moment.

And then, as if on cue, he groaned, pulling away just enough to flop back against the couch cushion.

"I'm starving," he muttered, rubbing his hand over his face. "Make me something?"

I smirked, still catching my breath. "You're always starving."

"And you always feed me," he shot back, grinning like he already knew he'd won.

So I got up, pulling his hoodie around me, and padded to the kitchen.

Chicken sausages. Toasted bread. Some juice.

Nothing fancy. But it was always enough for him.

When I was tossing the chicken sausages, he said, "That's not how it's supposed to be done. The flame should be high... you need to toss the pan like this."

I couldn't stop laughing.

He took over, full of confidence, and when he was finally done tossing, he flipped them onto his plate with flair.

Then he took a bite—and the inside was completely raw.

I burst out laughing, teasing him mercilessly.

He rolled his eyes while I put the sausages back into the pan and cooked them properly.

He sat at the counter while I cooked, hair still messy, shirt back on but half-buttoned.

He talked while I worked, about nothing in particular—his meetings, new movie release, how he needed a break.

And I listened. Sometimes I chimed in. Sometimes I just let the sound of his voice fill the room because it was a sound I hadn't realized I missed so much.

We ate standing at the counter, passing the juice glass back and forth between bites.

He finished first, as usual, then leaned in to kiss my temple as I chewed on the last piece of toast.

His hand slid down my back, resting there for a minute longer than it needed to.

"I have to go," he said, regret thick in his voice.

"Me too," I replied.

We both had work. Deadlines. Places to be.

But neither of us moved right away.

We stood there, too close to be casual, not close enough to stay.

At the door, he kissed me again.

Soft. Quick. But it lingered in all the places that mattered.

"Soon?" he asked quietly.

"Soon," I promised.

I'll text you. He said

And then he was gone.

I locked the door, leaning my forehead against it for a second, breathing in the ghost of him still left in the room.

Already counting down the time until we could steal another morning like this.

Because these were the moments that made all the noise and waiting in between worth it.

Even if they never felt like enough.

THE LOVE THAT LINGERS

Love that lingers like smoke in the skin,
A fire within that burns quiet, not thin.
Come what may, through time or test,
I'll remember him smiling, and feel my chest
Fill with the echo of what we once knew—
May he linger in me, 'til my last breath too.

Some stories don't end. They soften. Stretch thin over time. But they never quite disappear.

They live in the spaces between what was said and what wasn't, between moments lived and the ones still replayed when no one's watching.

Some loves aren't loud. They just… linger.

We keep meeting. Once a month. Sometimes twice or thrice. Sometimes not at all.

Weeks pass, life happens-work, family, responsibilities, the things we both chose long before we chose each other.

But distance has never mattered to us. It still doesn't.

Because when we meet—when he steps through the door or I step into his car— it's like time folds in on itself.

Familiarity settles in like a well-worn rhythm. And there we are. Not starting over. Just continuing.

I don't know if this is right or wrong. Maybe I'm not ready to figure that out. Maybe I never will be. All I know is that with him, there's no performance. No masks.

I don't have to edit myself. Or hold back the softer, messier parts.

With him, I am easy. Known. Enough. Maybe that's what love is. Not certainty, but space. The kind where you can be vulnerable without fear. Where silence doesn't demand to be filled. Where you are seen—and still safe.

There's a song he plays quite often when we are together. He always says it reminds him of me. And now, when I hear it—anywhere, everywhere—I think of him too. Of the first time we met. The way it didn't feel like the first time at all.

The song lingers on me long after it ends. But it follows us, like a shadow stitched to the edges of our time together.

The lyrics echo that feeling perfectly:-

"It didn't feel like the first time when I met you for the first time. It seemed as if you touched my heart's wounds and soothed them. I don't know the distinction between right and wrong, if you do, please let me know…"

And when we part, rushing back into our separate mornings, he always presses one last kiss to my forehead.

Like a quiet promise. And I always watch him walk away. Like a quiet prayer.

When will I see him next? I never know. Neither does he. But somehow, we always find our way back.

When I miss him too much, I find myself returning to his pictures—again and again. Each one a small resurrection. A stolen moment, still breathing. They make me smile, soft and slow. And sometimes, they ache. Because even captured in pixels, he feels near. Tangible. Like I could reach out and press my fingers to the screen and feel the warmth of his eyes staring back at me. Like memory made flesh, if only for a heartbeat.

We don't have a single picture of us together. And maybe that's how it was meant to be. Some things are better left to memory—to the echo of laughter in empty rooms, to the hush of nights when music takes over and the world feels paused. Some things live better in the spaces we keep sacred.

Every night, when I close my eyes and fold my hands in prayer, his name slips through my lips. Quiet. Almost an afterthought. A wish. For his safety. His happiness.

And—if I'm honest—for this. Whatever this is. To last a little longer. To keep lingering. Because I know he wants that too.

We have our own lives. Separate. Full. Complicated. But when we are together, we are happy. And maybe— for now—that's enough.

Sometimes life makes you selfish. You find something rare and keep it hidden from the world. Just so it doesn't get ruined. That's what we are. Something unspoken. Something that doesn't ask to be explained or approved.

Because this is the love that lingers.

The passion we have for each other moves like a tide—inevitable, pulling. I've never known this kind of fire. It lives not only in the touch, but in the nearness. In the way we hold each other in the quiet, drifting into sleep as if our hearts recognize the same rhythm.

There are moments when our love is slow—reverent, like a prayer whispered against skin. And then, there are moments when it rushes—hurried, hungry, urgent. Every version of it lingers. Each one a fingerprint left on the soul.

His cologne still lingers—on my pillow, in the folds of my clothes. Not as a memory, but as presence. Because he is not past. He is still here. Just not always in reach. And when I close my eyes, it's like he returns to me in scent—in breath—in the spaces between. Some things are not meant to vanish. Some things stay to remind you they never really left.

It stays with me. In quiet mornings, in the hush between his footsteps and the door closing behind him. In the soft brush of his hand as he's leaving. In the weight of his name in my prayers.

And in the knowing that even when we drift—we are never really gone from each other.

I used to think love came with a label. A checklist. A role to play.

But with Yash, there's no script. No map. And in that formlessness, there's ease.

A way of being that doesn't demand definition.

He doesn't complete me—I was never missing pieces.

But he sees me in ways that make me want to stay seen. With him, I don't need permission to be anything. I can be raw. Loud. Uncertain. Soft. And in my silences, he doesn't fill the space. He holds it.

He's healed parts of me I didn't even know were hurting. And still... some days, I wonder: What if the healing is never done?

What if love—the kind that lingers—also leaves?

I want to believe we'll survive whatever storms come. That even in the distance, we'll find each other again. But belief is strange. It bends. It waits. Sometimes, it breaks.

Right now though... we are here. And maybe that's all love really needs. Or maybe—it's the beginning of something else. Something I'm not ready to name just yet.

I don't think anyone is ever ready. Not really.

But when someone makes you feel alive again—like the parts of you that had gone quiet suddenly remember how to sing— It's kind of worth the risk.

And sometimes, late at night, when the world feels sharp and uncertain, I wonder—

What happens when lingering isn't enough anymore?

But I leave the question unanswered—like a pebble dropped into a quiet lake, rippling through me long after. Because right now, this is ours.

And sometimes… maybe that's what lingering truly means—not the grasp, but the grace. Not the holding on, but the returning. The showing up again and again, until presence itself becomes a prayer. A rhythm. A spell.

The love that lingers is the kind that threads through the unseen. That slips between time and breath, carrying you gently through all the in-between places the world forgets to name.

ACKNOWLEDGMENTS

To Sunita, whose quiet wisdom and profound presence transformed my understanding of love—your subtle yet powerful influence has illuminated my heart, making me truly believe in the beauty and depth of love.

To Tiara, my constant companion, my unwavering best friend—you've stood beside me through every chapter, both on and off these pages.

To Mita, whose persistent encouragement gave me the push I needed to finally complete this book—your belief kept me going.

To Sagar, for thoughtfully recommending Aishwarya, who introduced me to Uma and Agrima—your recommendations have enriched my journey immensely.

To Agrima and Uma whose insightful feedback and invaluable suggestions elevated my writing—your perspectives have made all the difference.

Thank you all for being an essential part of this journey.

ABOUT THE AUTHOR

Maya is a lifelong lover of literature who found her earliest inspirations within the pages of fiction and romantic storytelling. Though her youthful fascination with love and emotion shaped her inner world, life's demands led her down a different path—one that required resilience, independence, and strength.

A dedicated literature enthusiast, she has spent years honing her voice not only through reading and reflection, but also through the art of public speaking. Today, she mentors young students in effective communication and personal expression, inspiring them to find confidence in their own stories.

The Love That Lingers marks her literary debut—a poignant return to the world of fiction and a quiet reclaiming of the romance she once set aside. Through her writing, she explores the complex terrain of vulnerability, connection, and the truths we discover when we allow ourselves to be seen.